COULD REMO RESIST:

The golden forked tongues of Palmer Rizzuto and Schwartz—three attorneys with enough slimy savvy to tie Remo's muscle power into legal knots, and crucify him on the fine points of the law. . . ?

The luscious, lusting lips of Debbie Pattie—the sleaze queen of rock, with the voice millions would pay anything to hear, and the body any man would do anything to touch. . . ?

The busy, busy hands of Robert Dastrow—the terrifying tinkerer who used his monstrous mechanical ingenuity to turn the world into his playpen, and its entire population into his imminent victims. . . ?

Even with Remo's mentor Chiun on his side, the odds are bad—but now Chiun is ready to abandon his incorrigibly idealistic student in disgust, and the odds on the Destroyer not being destroyed are zero to none. . . .

____THE DESTROYER #66____

SUE ME

#66

The Destroyer

SUE ME

WARREN MURPHY & RICHARD SAPIR

A SIGNET BOOK

NEW AMERICAN LIBRARY

NAL BOOKS ARE AVAILABLE AT QUANTITY DISCOUNTS WHEN USED
TO PROMOTE PRODUCTS OR SERVICES. FOR INFORMATION PLEASE
WRITE TO PREMIUM MARKETING DIVISION, NEW AMERICAN
LIBRARY, 1633 BROADWAY, NEW YORK, NEW YORK 10019.

SIGNET, SIGNET CLASSIC, MENTOR, ONYX, PLUME, MERIDIAN
and NAL BOOKS are published by New American Library,
1633 Broadway, New York, New York 10019

First Printing, October, 1986

1 2 3 4 5 6 7 8 9

PRINTED IN THE UNITED STATES OF AMERICA

For Betty and Bill Grisham of Florida,
wonderful people and parents of super Nancy

It was easy money. Maybe too easy. But then there was no such thing. Someone was going to make a bundle out of this somehow, although Carl Schroeder couldn't figure out how.

He got free airfare to London and a hundred dollars when he arrived, and all he had to do was loosen a plate behind the coffeepot in the galley of the Gammon 787.

"There's dope there, right?" asked Carl. There was an angle to everything, and he usually found it.

"No. There's no dope there," said the man he could not see. The voice seemed to be coming from Carl's park bench. He knew the voice had been following him. It was nothing extraterrestrial though. Nothing ghostly. Just a normal sort of a voice whose owner said he wanted to be hidden. A voice he'd first heard in the lavatory of the poolroom on D Street.

Carl usually spent his mornings there. Pittsburgh was not much of a town in which to do anything else. Then again, in all his twenty-three years the world had not been much more to Carl than an endless series of poolrooms. He ran numbers for a while but the numbers bankers always demanded you show up at the same minute every day. It was worse than a full-time job.

He tried insurance fraud for a while but the third time he suffered whiplash in a single month, the insurance-company computers got the angle on him and he couldn't collect anymore.

Welfare was good, but Carl had made the mistake of listening to his teachers and staying in high school until graduation. If he were illiterate he might have been able to count on the City of Pittsburgh for pocket money. But when you were white and healthy and had a high-school degree, no welfare department would believe that.

And then there was that cursed workfare, which fortunately died under protest from civil-rights groups. Carl Schroeder shuddered to think he could have walked into an unemployment office in the morning and found a broom in his hand by afternoon.

The real problem with unemployment, a problem that Carl Schroeder saw and every commentator missed, was that you had to have a job before you could lose it and be eligible for benefits.

There was dope, of course. Big money in dope. But you could get killed dealing, or worse, be sent to jail for years. And in some jails you had to make license plates. Boring.

So when Carl Schroeder heard the voice in the lavatory telling him there was no work involved, he didn't believe it.

"Carl. There is no one here. I can see you but you can only hear me," came the voice.

Carl checked the booths. He peered behind the cracks in the mirror. He looked under the sinks. No microphones. No cameras. But the voice kept coming.

"Carl, you're not going to find any device. The way I do this is beyond your understanding. You would've had to take physics in high school. Somehow I do not believe you would do so much work in high school as to take physics."

"Who're you?"

"Someone who wants to give you a free trip to London and a hundred dollars to boot."

"Nobody gives something for nothing," said Carl.

"My business is my business," came the voice.

"You want me to carry a little package, right? Screw you. I ain't doin' no dope deal for a hundred bucks and a plane ticket. No dope deal, no way."

Carl examined the corners of the lavatory carefully. Cameras were often hidden in the corners, he had heard. Sometimes behind mirrors. But he knew there was no way to hide a camera behind the mirrors in this lavatory because there was solid concrete there. He had checked that a long time ago, because payoffs would often be left behind mirrors in public lavatories. While he had only found ten dollars once in what must have been fifteen thousand tries, it was still ten dollars and it sure was not work.

"Carl, this is not a dope deal, and you are no more going to figure it out than you can figure out where the voice is coming from."

"So what's your angle?"

"My angle is my angle, Carl. All you have to do is unscrew two simple Phillips screws."

"And then someone else comes along and picks up the coke or smack, right?"

"I told you, this is not a dope deal."

"Blow it. You're dealing with Carl Schroeder, not some bumpkin from Wheeling." To Carl, Wheeling,

West Virginia, represented the height of backwardness.

But later the voice was back, this time from an empty car outside. It pointed out that Carl had nothing to do for a while. He would get a free luxurious meal on the plane and all the champagne he could drink. He was going to go first class.

"Hey, if you're going to spend so much on first class, why not give me the difference and send me tourist?"

"I have my reasons for things. I understand things you don't," came the voice from the empty car. "I understand how things work."

"Bugger off," said Carl Schroeder.

By the time he reached the park he was hungry and when the voice started coming from an empty bench, the thought of a first-class meal was more attractive to him.

"If I say yes, what do I have to do exactly? I mean exactly."

"Exactly is the only way I work, Carl. When you are over the Atlantic, as the plane begins its descent into Heathrow Airport outside of London, you will take a Phillips screwdriver I will provide, and you will proceed to the rear galley, which services the tourist-class passengers. There you will see a coffeepot. Wait until the flight attendants are working the aisles, move the pot to the left and you will see a metal plate behind it. The first screw opens the plate. The next screw behind the plate holds an aluminum rod. Turn that screw two times to the left, replace the plate, replace the coffeepot in front of it. Go back to your seat and wait until the plane lands, whereupon you will be provided with your hundred dollars and a return ticket."

"I ain't takin' out no insurance policy on my life."

"This is no insurance scam, Carl."

"All right, where's the ticket?"

"Carl, do you really think I would give you a ticket worth eight hundred dollars so you could sell it? The one thing you have to remember about me is that I know how things work. You get your ticket just as you board. I already have your reservation."

"What about the screwdriver?"

"Look under the bench, Carl. Feel around."

Carl Schroeder moved a hand under the wood planking of the park bench, feeling the rough underside until his hand came to tape and a small cylinder. He ripped it out. It was shiny and dark and had a pocket clip.

"Hey, this is a fountain pen."

"Take off the cap, Carl," came the voice from the bench. The voice was somewhat squeaky.

Carl unscrewed the cap, and there looking at him was the crossed head of a Phillips screwdriver.

"Put the cap back on, Carl. By the way, you can only get a buck for it if you sell it on the street, so don't even bother."

"Hey, you've accused me of a lot of low dirt here," said Carl.

"No," came the voice. "I only know how things work. And I know how you work."

"Don't I need papers or something? One of them passport things?"

"Not this trip, Carl. Everything's been taken care of. I don't forget things, Carl. So don't worry about anything. You're the right man for this. Remember, I know how things work."

"Yeah, well look. If I'm gonna be working for you . . ."

"Not work, Carl. Don't ever think of it as work," came the voice.

"Good. 'Cause I don't relate well to labor. How do you get your voice to come out of things when you ain't there?"

"If it will make you feel better, Carl, I'll explain. Voices are sound waves. These waves can be directed. If you direct them with intensity, any metal object will resonate with the waves. That's how it is done."

"Okay for the voice. But how do you hear me and see me if I don't see no camera or mike?"

"That is more complicated, Carl. Better hurry."

"What for?"

"Your flight to New York is leaving in a half hour."

"I ain't goin' to New York."

"That's where you get your flight to London."

"How'm I gonna get out to the airport?" asked Carl, who suddenly noticed a yellow cab slowing down just outside the park.

"That's your taxi, Carl."

"Give me the money. I'll get my own cab."

"If you had fifteen dollars in your pocket now, you wouldn't even be listening to me, much less willing to take a plane ride. I know how things work, Carl, believe me. That's my problem. Always has been. There's your cab, hurry up."

So Carl Schroeder, in the bloom of his twenty-third year with less than a quarter in his pocket, boarded the waiting cab for a flight to London. At least he would eat well, and that as much as anything kept him going. The voice was right. If he had fifteen dollars he would have had himself a hot dog, gone back to the poolroom, and tried to parlay the remainder into serious drinking money.

The cabdriver knew even less than Carl about what was going on. All he knew was that he was paid half in advance to pick up Carl and would get the other half after he left him at the airport.

On the flight to New York, Carl ate a sandwich and cadged an extra drink. But on the flight to London aboard the Gammon 787, there was nothing to cadge. Everything was given to him. All the champagne he wanted. Filet mignon. A second meal of lobster. Playing cards. Magazines. Silver worth pocketing, and a doozy of a saltshaker.

As the pilot announced they would shortly begin their descent into Heathrow, Carl knew the time had come to do his work. Grumbling about the demands of life, he left the first-class cabin and made his way down the tourist aisles. He noticed how much more crowded the seats were, how much more tired the travelers appeared.

As the voice had predicted, the flight attendants were busy in the aisle. Carl saw the coffeepot, a drip affair that kept a bowl of the dark liquid warm on a heater. Gingerly he moved it to the side, and as the voice had predicted, there was the Phillips-head screw.

He snapped out the cylinder that looked like a fountain pen, unscrewed the cap, and inserted the head of his screwdriver. A perfect fit. Several quick turns to the left and the screw came undone. He presed his hand against the almost seamless plate and it moved to the side.

Despite the voice being correct about everything so far, Carl still expected to see a little plastic bag of white powder. He didn't. Just the aluminum pipe with the Phillips screw. He turned it two times to the left, moved back the plate, replaced the screw, covered it with the pot, and feeling worn out from more work than he'd done in a month, returned to his first-class seat at the front of the plane.

Yes, he told the flight attendant, he would like one more glass of champagne. "I deserve it. A little reward for myself, so to speak, ma'am."

Then he noticed the first mistake the voice had made. There was a little white card on a tray beside the champagne glass and it was his landing card. He had to fill in his passport number.

He didn't have a passport. The voice had said he didn't need one.

"When you were ticketed didn't they ask to see it?"

"That all happened before I got to the ticket booth. They had everything waiting for me."

"Gracious. Let me speak to the purser. You can't pass through customs without a passport," said the flight attendant.

And I probably won't get my hundred bucks in London, either, thought Carl. He was so enraged at the voice that he was tempted to return to the rear of the plane and turn back the screw. Carl Schroeder at that moment realized another thing about honest labor. You could get cheated out of its rewards.

On the way back to him, the flight attendant seemed to jump slightly, as though a passenger had goosed her. But then Carl saw everyone seem to jump. The plane was bucking, bucking so hard that it threw everyone in the aisles to the floor, and then with a sickening lurch hurled every person not buckled in to the ceiling.

Carl would have heard the screams better if he weren't screaming so hard himself.

But the voice was right after all. He did not need his passport when he got to England. He arrived in the English countryside at three hundred fifty miles an hour and, like everyone else in first class and right back to the last four rows of the tourist section, was met not by a customs clerk but by hard English rock.

It was one of the worst air disasters ever, at a time of an increasing number of air disasters, and even before the grieving had begun the lawyers arrived to reap their sustenance from the blood on the ground.

Foremost was the famous Los Angeles negligence firm of Palmer, Rizzuto & Schwartz. They not only got to the wealthiest families first, but they also provided the best initial case. They could prove beyond a shadow of a doubt that the Gammon 787 had faulty ailerons. They were backed by the best witness in the business, engineer Robert Dastrow, a man so brilliant that even the high-priced lawyers of airlines and construction firms could never discredit him.

It was said of Robert Dastrow that he knew the company's product better than their own engineers. It was said of Palmer, Rizzuto & Schwartz that on the day the world ended, they would have Earth as their client and would begin legal proceedings against Almighty God.

Even the best negligence lawyers, those unused to taking second place to anyone, tended to back away when the awesome might of this gigantic law firm moved into a case. Airlines and plane manufacturers trembled when they heard the names Palmer, Rizzuto & Schwartz.

Besides the major industrialists on the flight, whose lives and services were worth millions, there was even a good case for a ne'er-do-well from Pittsburgh, Carl Schroeder. One of the many junior attorneys working for Palmer, Rizzuto & Schwartz had found an aunt of the boy, and had guaranteed he could prove a loss in a British court, a substantial monetary loss.

His case against Gammon and its failure to properly secure the aluminum aileron-stabilization bar was that they had deprived this aunt of Carl's monumental potential in life. Why was it so monumental? Because, as the attorney intoned to the jury, young Carl hadn't used any of it yet.

The cost of Gammon 787's went up as the awards mounted and every new Gammon was recalled to resecure the aluminum aileron-stabilization bar and make access to it more difficult.

In Paris, France, a young art student pining for Seattle, Washington, made a strange, no-questions-asked deal. She would get her airfare home, provided she smoked a cigarette in a strange place.

She was a good deal shrewder than Carl Schroeder, the Pittsburgh hustler. She was not going to smoke that cigarette in the rear of the plane until it landed. And she didn't want a hundred dollars upon landing. And she also had her passport. And she did most certainly care about possibly harming the lives of others.

So only when everyone was debarking in Seattle from the French jet did she go to the rear lavatory, take two puffs of her cigarette, and put it out in the disposal bin loaded with used paper towels. She was not prepared for how quickly the jet went up in flames, and barely got out with her life.

Francine Waller was torn between going to the police and trying to keep herself out of trouble. She knew now, with the quick combustion of the plane, that she would have been dead along with everyone else on board if the plane had not already landed and discharged most of its passengers.

She did not sleep well for several nights, but what changed her mind, swung it over to the side of the law, was the talking brass bedpost. It was the same voice that had talked to her in Paris and told her how she could get home and make a hundred dollars to boot.

"You didn't earn your airfare, Francine," came the voice.

"I know how voices can be beamed and use metal as speakers. I looked it up after we talked the last time."

"So you know that."

"I do."

"You didn't follow instructions."

"I'd be dead if I did. The material on the plane seats was like kindling. It went right up."

"Yes, I know how those things work. Unfortunately I misjudged you. Some people are so strange. They're not as simply designed as airplanes."

"So what do you want from me?"

"I want you to forget about how you got back home, and I will forget about you."

"You would have murdered an entire planeload of people. Are you a spy?"

The voice laughed from the brass bedstand in Francine Waller's Seattle home.

"What's so funny?"

"A spy works for a government. Spies are killed by other spies. Governments don't work well at all; therefore I don't work for governments."

"Leave me alone, and I'll leave you alone," said Francine.

"I do hope that's so. You know, you disappointed me mightily."

"If living does that, I'm afraid I'm going to try to disappoint you for a long time to come."

"Remember, if your conscience gets the better of you, it's your life that's at stake."

"It's the only thing that's keeping me from the police," said Francine.

"Thanks for letting me know how you work," came the voice.

In the following days, Francine became despondent. She thought of what might have happened to her and everyone else on board. She thought of that person who might have murdered others doing it again. She even heard of a similar disaster in Mexico where more than a hundred people died in the flames of the burning jet, fueled by the seats that had not been changed despite the Seattle fire.

She read that a law firm, Palmer, Rizzuto & Schwartz, was calling this failure to change seat material "gross negligence" of the worst sort.

"They had ample proof in Seattle that their planes were death traps and yet they did nothing. The American public cannot be subjected to such negligence by airplane manufacturers who do not care about their product once it has left the assembly line," said a spokesman for Palmer, Rizzuto & Schwartz. "Seattle was a lesson to everyone in the world except, it seems, the manufacturers. A jury that values life must make the air safe for travel by insisting through a significant penalty that human life is more valuable than a few dollars saved on seat cushions."

But Francine Waller knew who was really responsible. She was. If she had reported what she had done, the second aircraft might not have gone up in flames.

And she couldn't live with that. She couldn't live with knowing that she could have saved lives but chose instead to keep herself comfortable. Even the new motorbike she had won in a contest she didn't remember entering failed to console her. Nothing was worth anything until she cleared her conscience.

So she took her new Yamasaki motorbike with the teardrop gas tank and the super deluxe chrome exhausts and drove it to the police station. But on the only stretch of open highway, the bike picked up speed because the throttle jammed, and the brakes failed.

Francine thought at first of jumping off, heading the bike into a tree and saving herself. At fifteen miles an hour there would be a few broken bones. But the Yamasaki was up to twenty, and then thirty-five, a killing speed on a motorbike. By the time she was at fifty, Francine Waller was holding on for her life. At eighty-five miles an hour, when she had to make the most minor turn, the bike spilled her like a bag of potatoes flying unprotected into a concrete wall.

The only thing left unbroken was her crash helmet. Her neck snapped, four ribs jammed into her heart, and her spinal cord was so badly damaged that had she lived, she wouldn't have been able to wiggle anything below her chin ever again.

But her parents were not without recourse in the death of their precious daughter. An attorney for Palmer, Rizzuto & Schwartz, a famous Los Angeles negligence firm, said others had died in the same tragic way. They were handling the estate of a famous actor who had died on a Yamasaki just like the Wallers' daughter.

"It seems there is a retention ring on the throttle that has to be replaced or the bike in some cases just keeps on accelerating. In some cases the driver becomes a human cannonball. They are not safe machines."

"Isn't this ambulance-chasing?" the mother asked.

The young lawyer was smooth, as though he were rehearsed.

"You could call it that. And you'd be right. But look at who's doing the chasing. We're Palmer, Rizzuto & Schwartz and we redress the damages done by large corporations to otherwise helpless individuals. You can go to any lawyer you want. But no law firm has won as many judgments, large judgments, as we have. And I might add righteous judgments. Yamasaki knew they had problems, but they thought it was cheaper to pay off some small negligence suits than to change a design. And they will continue to operate like that if people don't make it too expensive for them to do otherwise. We don't think they should get away with it. And we don't think you should let them get away with it."

"Who are you?" asked the mother. "Palmer, Rizzuto, or Schwartz?"

"Neither, ma'am. I'm Benson, as I introduced myself. I find that many of the grieving don't even hear the name at first."

"Tell me, Mr. Benson, how many grieving homes have you entered?"

"It would be a lot fewer, ma'am, if the companies knew they had to pay more when they failed to take reasonable safeguards."

"How many, Mr. Benson?"

"I'm afraid I've lost count."

"Do you really believe that bull you've just given me?" said Francine's mother. It was too hard to listen to nonsense when her young daughter had been taken from her so abruptly. All her illusions of a nice world had ended at Francine's grave.

"We've got this company cold. We can do the best job. We won't charge you a penny, but only do it on contingency."

"And how much for taking the case on contingency?"

"Fifty percent."

"Isn't thirty usual?"

"We get more for you at fifty percent than you'd get at seventy percent with someone else. Palmer, Rizzuto & Schwartz has a record of securing judgments almost twenty percent above the national average."

"You're a damned vulture, young man. But I suppose the grieving now require vultures. All right. I agree. Make them pay for Francine."

"You won't regret it," said young Mr. Benson.

It was not a major transaction for a firm as large as Palmer, Rizzuto & Schwartz. But it was recorded by a secretary whose job was to enter all new accounts in her computer. Strangely, it also required her to list the time and date a lawyer was sent to the stricken family, when the assignment was given, and who made it.

She never knew why this was required of her, and in a firm as large as Palmer, Rizzuto & Schwartz, no one noticed a lowly secretary performing yet another computer function, especially since most of the employees didn't understand how the computer system worked anyway, and those who did assumed either Mr. Palmer or Mr. Rizzuto or Mr. Schwartz had asked for it.

And so Francine's death and the date and time of her mother's subsequent retention of a lawyer went into the computer. And of course, no one knew someone was taking the information out. No one knew it went into a central file and became a statistic. And this statistic would have made the young lawyer proud of his ability to sell the services of the firm.

The statistics also showed that so effective was Palmer, Rizzuto & Schwartz that it had put several firms into bankruptcy. It was a symptom of a national problem. America had become so litigious that some industries faced imminent collapse. In hospitals, specialties were dying because it was too expensive for doctors to bear the skyrocketing cost of malpractice insurance. Obstetrics, the bringing of babies into the world, might very well disappear as a practice in America. But it was not a crisis yet and the man looking at the statistics felt he was not sure how to cope with it.

Anyway, Harold W. Smith, head of top-secret CURE, had more important problems. His killer arm had gone insane.

2

His name was Remo and he didn't care if anyone thought he was crazy. He had just realized the world was crazy. Maybe he was the only sane man in the universe. He didn't care about being the only one. He did care about staying sane.

Remo made sure the oven was lit before he went through the house looking for the person to put into it. It was a simple two-story frame house in Chillicothe, Ohio, but it had a few added attractions. Like trapdoors. Secret chambers carved into supporting beams. Double walls to hide behind.

Dope dealers had used it for a while until it was occupied by a petty criminal named Walter Hanover, who had most recently acted as a go-between for a kidnapped boy and his parents. Somehow law-enforcement authorities had bungled the ransom and the parents were out $300,000 and the boy was gone. Remo had seen the weeping parents on television, saying they had mortgaged everything to get their son back and now there was nothing left to lure the kidnappers. No law could touch Walter Hanover even though he now sported a new red convertible, yet had no visible means of support.

Walter's new convertible was sitting proud and shiny in the driveway when Remo approached Walter's house despite all warnings from upstairs about how insane all this was, that he had no business in this affair.

Walter Hanover sat on the porch smoking a strange cigarette that seemed to make him exceptionally mellow.

Remo put his right hand on the fender.

"Hey, man, fingers leave prints. That's fresh polished," said Walter Hanover.

Remo smiled. He closed his fingers ever so smoothly, sensing the metal under the pads, knowing each finger ridge could collect tiny particles of polish, hearing a tiny squeaking as the flesh compressed first the polish, then the paint, then the metal under the paint until there was a crack so loud it felt like steel wool scrubbing the eardrums, and Walter Hanover clasped his hands to his ears and then shook his frizzy blond head in astonishment. The right fender of his shiny new car looked as though someone had grabbed a handful of it and crushed it like children's clay.

Standing beside it with a maniacal smile was a dark-haired man in his early thirties. There was nothing exceptional about him. He was thin, with thick wrists, dark eyes, high cheekbones, wearing a dark T-shirt and light pants, and very casually with his right hand he had crushed the right-front fender of Walter Hanover's new convertible.

"Hi," said Remo.

"Whadya do that for?"

"So when I tell you I am going to stuff you into your oven, you'll believe me."

"Wait here," Walter said, and disappeared into

the house. It was a wooden house and therefore gave off undistorted vibrations. Metal warped sound. The cells in wood purified it. These very light sound waves that people thought they didn't really hear gave them the illusion of knowing someone was in their house by extrasensory perception.

But there was nothing extrasensory about it. People were just not aware of those senses, or rather never learned to be.

Remo had been trained over the years so that now he knew he walked among people who had never been introduced to their bodies, dead bodies, unused bodies, improperly used bodies, clogged with the fat of animals, distracted by worry, overwhelmed by fear, slogging along using less than eight percent of everything available to them.

So Remo knew the house and the ground he stood on and knew Walter Hanover had not fled through a rear window but was hiding somewhere in the house.

"Coming, Walter," Remo called out pleasantly, and walked up the steps to the porch, and waited listening to the wood in the house reverberate with his coming. Then he went into the kitchen and turned on the oven.

"Walter, I'm turning on the oven," Remo sang out.

Remo glanced at the dials and the buttons. It was a new form of oven, made simple for the housewife who hated gadgets. Remo pressed the button to turn on the oven, and the grill light lit up. He pressed what he thought was the grill-light button and the timer went off. He pressed all the buttons and the oven announced it was cleaning itself.

Remo sensed a lot of heat coming from the oven,

and that was good enough. He was not going to bake
a cake, after all.

"Walter, I'm coming. Ready or not. Here I come,"
Remo sang out. He paused a moment, and his senses
drew him to the second floor. He moved swiftly up
the steps and found himself in a hallway with four
closed doors. He opened every door. The rooms
were furnished in pre-junk. Glass tables with wire-
backed chairs, and pottery lamps that looked more
like the solids from a septic tank than hand-molded
clay.

Walter was not hiding in any of the rooms. But he
was very close.

"I know you're here, Walter. Come on out. The
oven is ready for you."

Remo felt a rustling behind a wall with a picture of
the Statue of Liberty on it. Someone had framed
what had to be the worst movie poster ever made. A
man was hanging from the Statue of Liberty, and he
looked as stiff as a grade-school entry in an art show.
The body didn't go with the head, and the head
didn't go with the hands, and there were more people at the bottom of the poster getting their names
mentioned than on any other poster he had ever
seen. In fact this movie had more producers than
World War II or the fall of the Roman Empire.

Walter Hanover was hiding somewhere in the
wall under the picture. Obviously the picture hid
some button or lever. Remo pressed both palms against
the picture, steadied his breathing, and then simply
pushed the picture back through the wall as shards of
plaster and wood strips exploded into dust.

Walter Hanover cringed in the little once-hidden
crawl space behind the wall. Remo picked him up by
the neck.

"Got you," said Remo pleasantly.

"Hey, man, who are you? What are you?"

"I am the voice of righteousness. The good fellow doing the good deed. Your friendly helpful neighbor."

"You're crazy, right? I hear crazy men have incredible strength sometimes."

"I am the only sane man in the universe."

"Now I know you're crazy. Whaddaya want?"

"There's a boy missing. His family paid three hundred thousand dollars."

"They buy you?"

"Yes, they did."

"What'd they pay?"

"I think their taxes. They paid their taxes and they lived a good life and I think they deserve a good deal better than they got."

"You with the government?"

"In a way, yes."

"Then you can't touch me. I got my rights."

"Ah, my good man," said Remo, lifting Walter Hanover like luggage and carrying him with his feet trailing down the stairs like shirts that had been improperly packed. "You have a problem. I only sort of work for the government."

"You're crazy."

"Walter," said Remo when they reached the oven that was still cleaning itself, "you know where the boy is. I'm sure of it. I want to know."

"Hey, man, I don't have to testify. There's no law in the world that'll make me testify. And besides, that oven is locked because it's cleaning itself."

Remo punched a hole in the oven door big enough to fit Walter through. At that moment Walter Hanover, for the first time in his life, considered his civic duty. He liked Remo and he wanted to help.

"The problem is they got the kid down in Corsazo. They sold him to some brothel."

"Did you help?"

"No. No way. I swear. By my mother's sainted grave. There's no way to get the kid back. That's a foreign country."

"We'll see what we can do, won't we?"

"I hate foreign countries."

"Do you like roasted ass of Hanover?" asked Remo. Walter did not. Walter agreed to fly down to Corsazo with Remo, where Remo left Walter in a hotel room. Walter did not flee. Walter would have fled, but the thin man with the thick wrists named Remo had put pressure on the back of his neck in some strange way that made Walter's legs as flabby and useless as overcooked spaghetti.

"Just want to keep you here until I find the boy."

"This is Corsazo, man. They're gonna cut your throat. And then I'm gonna be stuck here."

"That's the least of your worries."

"Yeah, what's a worse worry, man?"

"That they don't cut my throat," said Remo.

Finding a brothel in Corsazo was like finding a hamburger at McDonald's. The small Mexican town served as a magnet for American vice. There was nothing Americans couldn't buy here, from children to cocaine. Anything the warped mind could desire, Corsazo provided. Consequently, because it gave some Yankees what they wanted, the Yankees thought of the residents as less than moral.

Nobody liked anyone else, and everyone got what they wanted.

Remo went to the first brothel. It looked like a hardware store, but instead of pots and machinery in the window there was a young woman, looking willing.

"I've come for a twelve-year-old boy. His name is Davey Simpson. He has dark hair, and he has been taken recently from America. He probably has bruises from being forced to work in a place like this."

"We can get you a nice twelve-year-old boy."

"I've come to take this one home."

"We can sell you a boy. A nice boy with skin so soft a duck would die of envy." This from the proprietor, a large woman who smelled of rum and perfume so strong it could overpower a garbage dump. Remo could almost see the particles of odor emanate from her too-ample breasts. She had a dark mustache.

"Do you have a bodyguard?" asked Remo.

"Are you going to cause trouble?"

"Absolutely," said Remo.

"Then you can take me on," said the woman, producing a stiletto with a point like an ice pick. She pressed it against Remo's jugular.

"That your safety pin?" said Remo.

"You want something I can give you, stay. If no, señor, I am afraid you must leave."

Remo flicked two fingers up under the ulnar artery of her knife hand, cutting off the blood flow as the knife flew away somewhere near the ceiling. He grabbed her neck like a dog collar and pressed her face into the glass of the store window. The young woman who sat there as advertisement fled, screaming. The madam was told either the glass or her face was going to give way any moment unless she told him the whereabouts of a new boy kidnapped in America and sold down here.

The bodyguard appeared from one of the back rooms. He looked short for his six feet, four inches because he was as wide around as he was tall. Masses of dark hair covered everything from his knuckles to his nose. He reached out to crush the thin American and went sailing back into the interior of the brothel with a crash to shake the building. His eyes rolled up into his head as his bladder released all over his shiny green pants, now somewhat shinier and darker from the moisture.

"Okay, Yankee. I do what I can," said the madam.

"No. You tell everyone down here that there is a mad American who has come for an American boy who was sold into slavery. Tell them this American is going to take the town apart, starting with the brothel owners and then the chief of police. Tell them that all their drug dealers will find their automatic weapons embedded in their intestines. If I don't have the Simpson boy by sundown, this town will cease to exist."

Thus spoke Remo. And naturally, when the madam quickly hurried to the bosses of the small city, they refused to believe such a threat. For that would mean accepting intimidation. And if there was one thing owners of whorehouses, dope cartels, and other forms of social malignancies could not tolerate, it was a threat to their authority. They knew better than anyone else that once people lost respect for their power they would be deposed by their own troops. So they sent a strong-arm team from several cocaine dealers, all armed with the latest American weapons, even grenade launchers.

There was much firing and many explosions around the brothel where they surrounded the American. Many of the leaders of the town bemoaned the public destruction. They even discussed making compensatory offerings to those who lost property.

When the firing died down and the hit men from the drug dealers failed to return, the leaders of the little city sent word to a Mexican Army post that an American was causing great damage to Mexican property.

While the Mexican Army, of course, was not as well equipped as the drug dealers' hit men, it considered itself somewhat better by virtue of valor. But even valor was no good against this amazing American, so they contacted the American consul, who apologized for the actions of his fellow countryman and took it upon himself to talk reason to the American.

The consul too did not return, and as the sun set bloody red in the west, the town leaders at last decided to produce the boy. As it turned out, he was still in training, being broken in to his new life.

Remo saw the welts on his back.

"Who did this to him?" he asked, feeling a rage that almost took away his balance, almost took away the powers he now had access to through his own, very different training.

A crone of a woman bent with age came forward.

"Who owns this house?" asked Remo.

Timidly, a well-dressed man in a white suit, Italian loafers, and one sedate gold chain around his neck emerged from a back room.

Remo buried both of them in the rubble of their brothel as the Simpson boy stood outside crying.

"It's all right," said Remo. "Your countrymen are here, son. You're going home."

Remo walked slowly down the main street with the boy, daring anyone to try to take him back. No one moved. The boy was afraid to be left alone, so Remo brought him to the hotel room where Walter Hanover sat with his spaghetti legs.

"That's him. That's one of them," said the Simpson boy.

"We'll just let him stay down here this way," said Remo.

"Ain't I gonna get better?" asked Hanover.

"No, as a matter of fact," said Remo, "you're going to get worse. Your legs will atrophy and it will creep up your spinal column."

Remo felt Davey Simpson tug his arm.

"Mister, I don't want to hurt anyone. I just want to go home. Don't do whatever that is to him."

"Okay," said Remo, and asked the Simpson boy to stand outside while he fixed up Walter Hanover. When the door was shut, Remo broke Hanover in two over his knee like a piece of kindling, leaving him for the city of Corsazo to bury.

"His legs won't be any worse than the rest of him," Remo told the Simpson boy on the way to the airport.

Remo delivered the boy just before dawn the next day. His parents couldn't believe their good luck. The mother stood dumbfounded for a moment and then in a rush of tears grabbed her son, hugging him as though she could make sure by the firmness of her grasp that he would never be stolen again. The father looked to Remo.

"How can we say thank you?" he asked.

"I should thank you."

"What for?"

"For giving me a chance to feel human again," said Remo.

At CURE headquarters hidden behind the cover of Folcroft Sanitarium in Rye, New York, the full impact of Remo's insanity was churning up out of the computer terminal. Not only had he risked exposure (there were several good identifications of him), but single-handedly he threatened U.S.-Mexican relations and brought enough attention to himself for foreign governments to wonder if America had a secret weapon.

They would not wonder for long because now foreign intelligence services would be looking for that weapon. Remo had done what he should never do. He had brought CURE dangerously close to exposure, and more than a decade ago CURE had gone to herculean efforts to arrange a phony execution for him just to have a man who no longer existed be the sole killer arm of the organization that could not exist.

For if it became known that America had set up an organization for its own survival working outside the Constitution, it would seem that the great experiment in democracy had failed. This could never be allowed to happen.

And now, for nothing that had anything to do with national security, Remo had endangered them all. And Harold W. Smith was furious.

His computers intercepted the horrible tale as the State Department tried to quiet down the uproar. Remo (it had to be Remo, no other person in the world could have done what had been done except his teacher, Chiun, who was Oriental and therefore did not fit the description) had gone into a country friendly to America and had taken it upon himself to terrorize it until his demands were met. He imposed his morality on a friendly country. He killed and maimed and damaged in said country and then dared anyone in the town to come after him as he walked slowly down the main street. He boarded a plane with a person as yet unproved to be an American citizen, looking Mexican soldiers in the eye and daring them to shoot. Then he flew back to America.

Apologies from everyone in the State Department were now flowing to the Mexican government.

When Smith finally heard from Remo he had only one question.

"Why?"

"I felt like it."

"That's it?"

"That's it," said Remo into the phone after he had dialed the special number that automatically scrambled sound waves so the line could not be tapped.

"You know what you endangered, of course."

"Not a damn thing, Smitty," said Remo. "Not a damn thing worth a damn, and especially not the organization."

"Remo, we may not be able to use you anymore," said Smith.

"Wonderful," said Remo.

"Do you still love your country?"

"That's just why I did what I did."

"Remo, we've got to talk about this. We've got to talk in person. I think you've got to understand how much your country needs you now."

And then Smith heard what he had thought he would never hear from Remo, the person he sometimes thought of as the last true patriot:

"I need me, Smitty," said Remo and hung up, leaving America without the killer arm of its last hope for survival, as one president once called CURE. Another chief executive had called it the nation's ace in the hole. Now it was no more deadly than the microchips in the computers at headquarters in Folcroft.

Remo did not feel very good about hanging up on Smith. He respected the man. He trusted the man. But too much had gone down and nothing ever seemed to improve in America, while an awful lot seemed to get worse. He just wanted to do what was right. Just once. Not what was secret. Not what was secure. Not what was in some grand plan for the United States of America, but something for an American family.

And he felt good again.

Harold W. Smith knew from the phone call that Remo was somewhere in Ohio. He put the investigation of Palmer, Rizzuto & Schwartz on hold while he drove up to Connecticut, where he knew Remo eventually had to return. But if he had known what the law firm was planning, he would have stayed at his computers.

Chiun, Master of Sinanju, glory of the House of Sinanju, teacher of Remo, the first Sinanju assassin to set foot on the shores of the new country called the United States and therefore written in the history of the House of Sinanju as the discoverer of the United States, prepared to receive Harold W. Smith, head of CURE.

As discoverer of this country, Chiun had the obligation to future Masters of Sinanju to describe the nature of the people, and how to deal with them.

It was thus somewhat amusing to Chiun to hear Smith describe Remo as suffering some mental imbalance, "emotional chaos without reason."

These were the exact words, in Korean of course, that Chiun had used to describe the American character, Smith in particular.

It was the only explanation of why Smith would

assure gold tribute delivered to Sinanju, and then
not have Chiun or Remo eliminate the current emperor, called President, to install himself or a relative on the throne. Instead, he had Remo and Chiun
running around the world performing the strangest
feats, and then even when they were wildly successful, insisting they remain secret. Acts that would
have resounded to anyone's glory. Feats Chiun was
proud to list in the history of Sinanju, which in the
course of things would survive this crazy young nation.

The United States was a mere two hundred years
old. Rome was a thousand years old when it fell. But
Sinanju, sun source of all the martial arts, outlived
them all, every dynasty it had ever served. Every
empire and every kingdom. It was forty-five hundred
years old, and even though it was not written in the
histories of Sinanju, Chiun was sure other Masters of
Sinanju listened to other emperors just as insane.
There was of course a formula for dealing with similar situations, and Chiun did not even have to think
to use it.

"Your words are like the sun itself, casting illumi-
nation upon the darkness of souls," said Chiun in his
night velvet kimono, with characters from the main
ung poem embroidered in gold thread upon it. His
long fingernails were resting delicately in his lap.
Wisps of hair flowed down his cheeks and brushed
his parchment-dry skin.

"I don't know what to do with Remo."

"It is a wise master," said Chiun, "who comes to a
devoted servant."

Why Smith never ordered Chiun to appear at his
place of residence, Chiun did not know. But if Smith
chose always to visit Chiun and Remo in some out-of-
the-way place, that was just more evidence of his

peculiarity, another piece in a mosaic of madness that was so much a part of this country and unfortunately sometimes still affected Remo.

Smith sat rigid on a chair, his briefcase resting on his lap. He wore his usual gray three-piece suit and Dartmouth tie and his expression was dour, not because of the problem at hand but because that was always his expression. Chiun attributed it to his bad breathing technique, but Remo said it was the man's soul showing through his face. Despite comments like that from Remo, Chiun knew Remo respected Smith, and they shared some sort of white bond that Chiun did not quite understand, an irrational loyalty to what they called their country.

"I don't know what's gotten into Remo, but yesterday he took it upon himself to go down to a village in a friendly country and terrorize it. And why? There was no strategic or tactical reason for any of it. It had nothing to do with what we have been commissioned to do."

Chiun nodded gravely.

"Yes, Remo has done some strange things from time to time, but I have always understood them," continued Smith. "He's a good man with a good heart."

"He speaks nothing but praises of his Emperor Smith. His lips lie fallow but that they sing your glory."

"But the other day, all I heard was that he was going to correct something. There was this family in Ohio who had lost a son."

"Ah," said Chiun. He remembered it. He had watched with Remo on the television in the Westport home that CURE had bought for them after Remo had complained about living in so many hotels.

Chiun remembered a large sum being mentioned. It was a traditional ransom, quite common throughout history, but in the hands of the lunatic Americans, something that turned into a fiasco. Not only had the abductors been paid the money, but they had failed to return the child, something any self-respecting kidnapper even during the worst days of the Chinese warlords would never do.

If one took ransom and did not return the victim, how could one demand ransom again? Yet in this country, according to American tradition, the police had stepped in and predictably, the parents lost their money and their child.

It was perhaps too great a hope for Chiun's aged breast, but he wondered if Remo at last was seeking gold. In this land supposedly filled with people who did nothing but lust for wealth, Chiun had found more people who refused to do things for money than in any other country on earth in all history. Those who prided themselves on their religious motivation were the worst offenders.

For professional assassins this weakness could be ruinous, and while Remo had learned what no other white in all history and only a few from Sinanju had ever learned, he could not quite unlearn his early habit of not caring about the rightful assassin's tribute. When Chiun had demanded Remo's tribute be included with the gold shipped to Sinanju, Remo had insanely answered:

"Okay. If you want it. You never spend the damned stuff anyhow. The House of Sinanju has mint-fresh coins from Cyrus the Great of Persia."

"That does not matter," Chiun had said. "It is a question of what is right and what is wrong."

"Okay. Take the gold," Remo had said.

And was it any wonder, therefore, that when the treasures of Sinanju were stolen, Remo was off somewhere supposedly saving the world? What the world had ever done for Remo, Chiun did not know. It had done even less than this country he said he loved.

Now Chiun listened with some faint hope that at last Remo had learned some respect for the proper tribute. His heart quickened as he heard Remo had gone to the place where the boy was taken and found someone who had apparently colluded in the abduction.

Then he went down to those who had taken ransom and not returned the child and visited wrath upon them. So far so good, thought Chiun. And then, perfectly concluding the mission, he returned the child to the parents, this despite Smith's babbling about some form of national security and friendly-neighbor policy. Even better.

"Pray tell, O gracious Emperor, how much did Remo take in tribute from these people who had been violated in your kingdom?"

"Money?" asked Smith.

"Yes, that is what is used in America. How much in money was their tribute, a tribute I might add which would reflect to your glory also since I am led to believe your area does cover this entire country."

"Oh, he didn't take money," said Smith.

"He didn't? What did he take?"

"He said it made him feel good."

Chiun, whose breathing was tuned to the center of the entire universe, now felt the very tips of his lungs quiver in horror at what he feared had transpired.

"What," asked Chiun, "made him feel good?"

"Doing what he did. Returning the boy. Now, I can see getting emotionally—"

Chiun did not listen to the rest of the sentence. He could see Remo now, having performed in complete accord with the traditions of Sinanju, using all the techniques of the sun source of all the martial arts, breaking the will of an entire city, returning the kidnapped one home in triumph, and then doing absolutely nothing but feeling good about it.

"Why did he do it? Why did he do such an insane thing?" asked Chiun, his voice rising in anguished frustration.

"I don't know," said Smith. "I hoped you knew."

"How would I know? I'm not white. What could have made him do such a thing? What on earth could have made him do such a foolish thing?"

When Remo finally got home, he found something very rare had happened. Both Smith and Chiun, two men from cultures as far away as time and space could allow in this world, were for the first time agreeing on something.

Remo had acted insanely.

Remo stuck out his tongue and gave them both a razzing. He hadn't felt this good in a long time.

3

Joe Piscella and Jim Wiedman did not expect to die that day when they brought their lunch pails filled with beer and sandwiches to work. By their own choosing, they led simple lives. Both had served in Vietnam and both had decided that construction work paid well and you didn't bring it home to bed with you like other jobs. When you left your shovel or carpenter's gauge at the job, you didn't think about it until the next day.

After coming out of that war alive they had no desire to risk their lives again, so they insisted on never working on tall buildings or in tunnels. Life, they would say, was too precious to risk. Their wives agreed with them. They would rather do without a few things than have their husbands work with worry.

On the day Joe and Jim died, they were at one of the safest construction sites in the business. They were building a one-story auditorium, laying the cement roof along reinforced girders. When the tons of gray cement dried, the roof would be as secure as a bunker.

Jim thought they were laying too much too quickly. Joe said he didn't care. All he wanted was his onion sandwich and beer for lunch.

"If I wanted to worry about how much cement we was layin', Jim, I woulda gone for foreman. We do our job. We break for lunch. We do our job some more, buddy, and then we go home for supper."

Jim looked back toward the main sluices vomiting the gray lavalike cement into the loose molds above the reinforcing girders. The thing about cement, wet cement in particular, was that it was heavy. And the roof was wide, wider than any he had ever seen for cement. To his eye the girders did not seem strong enough.

The sun was hot this summer day in Darien, Connecticut, and he and Joe worked with their shirts off. It was the best time of year for construction. Work was plentiful and there was none of the draining numbness of the cold days of winter.

No one laid cement in winter, because in cold weather it didn't dry properly. And it was the drying that was so important.

"You hear something, Joe?" asked Jim.

"I hear the Yanks aren't gonna be in the playoffs this year," said Joe.

"No. Under your feet. The cement. The girders below. Don't you hear nothin'?"

"Hey, I don' listen to this. I don' think about this. I just do this. C'mon. What's the problem? We fall twenty feet if the whole thing goes. Big deal. Now whaddaya think of the Yanks last night?"

Jim looked out over the expanse of glistening wet cement. He could not remember so much being laid in one day. Usually they would do sections and let it dry and then build on that, because not only was dry cement strong, it was much lighter.

"Never mind the Yanks, for Chrissakes. Listen! Somethin's moving!"

Like many disasters, it looked at first like a harmless curiosity. The middle of the auditorium roof seemed to be turning into a whirlpool. A giant dimple formed in the center of the roof, and then, as though the cement were actually consuming itself from the center, the rest began to flow there, sucked in like water down the bathtub drain.

Joe and Jim were carried with that river. Their heavy boots caught instantly in the thick cement, and although the collapse of the wet cement skin on the roof appeared to be happening in slow motion, Joe and Jim moved even slower. It was impossible to run in wet cement.

Other workers tried to throw poles to them. Someone tried to get a crane to lower a beam they could grab. Everything happened so slowly, Joe even began to laugh at their awkwardness.

But as they got closer to the center and the beams beneath the cement began to crack under the suddenly shifting load, Joe realized what Jim had been screaming about for the last five seconds. They were going under.

In Darien that day, Jim and Joe did not get to their lunch. Instead they died horribly in a gooey gray mass, their lungs filled, their screams smothered, and their bodies sucked into the center of what was supposed to be the auditorium roof. It wasn't the fall that killed them. It was the breathing, or the lack of it. On that very dry day, surrounded by nothing but land, they drowned.

Even in their grief, the widows were glad to see the young attorney from a Los Angeles law firm which specialized in this sort of litigation, Palmer, Rizzuto & Schwartz. He knew exactly what the construction company had done wrong. Their husbands would be alive today if the company followed proper procedure. It was a perfect case of gross negligence.

"In America buildings are not supposed to collapse. This isn't Russia, where it happens all the time. This is America. Your husbands shouldn't have died."

At the company the engineers were dumbfounded. They couldn't figure out how it had happened. They knew they weren't supposed to lay cement over that broad an expanse all at once. And yet, somehow, every one of the daily construction orders called for that. It was as though some mysterious hand, a hand that knew exactly how the construction business worked, had cooked up a recipe for disaster.

The small company, already laden with debt, was going to be bankrupted by the lawsuit, not because they weren't covered by insurance. They were. But the next premiums would be so large that the firm would not be able to bid successfully on any future work.

In Los Angeles, in the shining new towers of Century Park City, the tragedy of Joe Piscella and Jim Wiedman was the first order of business at the offices of Palmer, Rizzuto & Schwartz. Nathan Palmer himself had called a meeting of the partners.

Palmer, Rizzuto & Schwartz had started out in a small storefront in Palo Alto, chasing ambulances for cases. They still kept the secondhand desk from their first office as a memento, encased in glass in their ultraluxurious, wall-to-wall-carpeted, football-field-size offices.

Nathan Palmer often referred to the desk as "our reminder of where we came from." Palmer, a graduate of one of the more prestigious Eastern law schools, played humble very well. Arnold Schwartz, who had barely gotten through one of the lesser law schools in California, never dared play humble. Arnold would tell passing cocktail waitresses the gross income of Palmer, Rizzuto & Schwartz. Arnold wouldn't drive to the drugstore in anything but his Rolls-Royce lest someone he would never see again might think he couldn't afford a Rolls.

And Genaro Rizzuto would go into poetic raptures about the desk. They were so poor, he would say, that this secondhand desk was almost repossessed and a collection agency actually was carrying the desk out the door when Rizzuto was listening to a judge award their first multimillion-dollar judgment.

The three partners never quite agreed on anything except the need for money. The millions they had made somehow didn't seem to make them free of money worries, but instead added to them.

Nathan Palmer, of good blond patrician looks, tended to marry often, and his divorces were always expensive. Genaro Rizzuto referred to gambling as "harmless entertainment" and could actually prove other hobbies were more expensive. Being a good lawyer, he could prove anything, but he had an ability to lose several hundred thousand dollars in a night, making Palmer's marriages and subsequent alimony settlements seem cheap by comparison. But the biggest financial disaster among the three partners was Arnold Schwartz.

At an early age Arnold had figured out an investment strategy of such complexity that a college math teacher suggested he make a career in physics instead of law.

This mathematical organization of the variations of the stock market kept Schwartz in a state of near-bankruptcy, barely able to sustain his Rolls-Royce and Beverly Hills mansion, both heavily mortgaged by loans. Because of the intricacies of his investment strategies, he was one of the few people who had managed to lose money in the boom markets of the early eighties.

Since Nathan Palmer, Genaro Rizzuto, and Arnold Schwartz had stopped using that plain scarred wooden desk back in Palo Alto, their personal money problems had increased to gigantic proportions. So when Palmer called a meeting of the partners, the other two came immediately. And they came yelling.

Rizzuto had been interrupted in the middle of a three-day poker game and was down almost a half-million dollars. He was sure his luck was going to change, and he immediately accused Palmer of being responsible for his inability to be able to recover his current losses.

Genaro Rizzuto was handsome, with a deep bronze California tan. He wore tight-fitting gray slacks, a sport shirt open to the navel, and enough gold chain around his neck to open a traveling jewelry store. He had one wife, to whom he gave anything she wanted except himself. They had honeymooned in Las Vegas and did not consummate the marriage until they returned to California. Sex was not high on Genaro Rizzuto's list of pleasures.

"What's going on?" demanded Rizzuto.

"Disaster," said Palmer. He wore a light summer suit with his Ivy League tie.

"So? Everything's a disaster. It could have waited. I was down, and just coming back. But you and your disaster stopped me. I'm owed for this, Nathan."

"Your half-million dollars is penny-ante compared to this," said Palmer. He held a report on a death-by-negligence case in Darien, Connecticut, that Palmer,

Rizzuto & Schwartz had just secured that morning, "We're all facing disaster. I don't know why we missed it before."

"What's we? You missed it. I never missed it," said Rizzuto, going to a glass bar set against a mirrored wall and pouring white wine into a Waterford crystal glass. Schwartz had insisted they buy expensive crystal even for the washrooms, lest by accident a plastic glass get transferred into an office and someone think they couldn't afford the good stuff.

"You don't even know what you missed?"

"What did I allegedly miss?" asked Rizzuto.

"That we're the biggest fools in the whole damned world," answered Palmer.

"How?"

"Wait for Schwartz," said Palmer.

Schwartz was delayed because he would not leave his house without his Rolex. He arrived looking as ever the epitome of prosperity. A dark three-thousand-dollar Savile Row suit fit his thin frame perfectly. Sedate but elegant horn-rim glasses made him appear thoughtful, and the gold Rolex just happened to appear from a cuff every few seconds as he adjusted one thing or another around his body.

"Don't tell me about disasters. I've just been on the phone with my broker."

"It's worse than the stock market."

"Nothing is worse than the market," said Schwartz.

"How the hell do you lose when everyone else is making money?" asked Rizzuto. He offered to get Schwartz a drink. Schwartz declined with a motion of his hand, the Rolex hand. He put his eight-hundred dollar Bazitti loafers on the long polished rosewood table and leaned back. Palmer could see the designer imprint on the bottom of the shoes. He was glad there was no such thing as expensive designer underwear; otherwise he would be in danger of being mooned by his partner.

Nathan Palmer did not like his partners. In fact, if he had met them in an elevator he would have gotten off at the wrong floor just to get away from them. But these were the men who had schemed with him to make Palmer, Rizzuto & Schwartz, and he never had any thought of going off alone. He might despise them personally, but professionally he respected their legal cunning.

"We have here the end of Palmer, Rizzuto & Schwartz. In Darien, Connecticut, we have secured a death-by-negligence case against a construction firm."

"It's insured, isn't it? We didn't go after something that wasn't insured," said Schwartz, who was an expert at freezing assets in danger of disappearing, a common occurrence when companies faced large judgments against them.

"Oh, it's insured," said Palmer.

"Then what's the problem?"

"The problem is the victims of this heinous crime of negligence—they were both smothered in concrete—were two common laborers, Joe somebody and Jim watchamacallit."

"So?" asked Schwartz.

"That's a three-hundred-thousand-dollar cap on their lives," Schwartz said. "That was the auditorium-roof construction, wasn't it?"

"Yes. Worked brilliantly," said Palmer.

"Who else was injured? Any engineers? A doctor, hopefully?" asked Rizzuto.

"Only the two laborers. Palmer, Rizzuto & Schwartz's share, gentlemen, should come to roughly three hundred thousand dollars."

"What's that after expenses?" asked Schwartz.

"A two-hundred-thousand-dollar loss. And Darien isn't all, there were the baby bottles. A perfect litigation against the company that produced the plastic wrong so it would shatter in the babies' mouths."

"That was a natural for any jury," said Rizzuto, who loved the gamble of facing a jury and wished the firm hadn't become so big that they never sent him out to plead a case anymore. "Babies with bleeding mouths. Hysterical mothers. Rich corporations."

"Except the life of a baby is never a seven-figure affair," said Schwartz. "And they suffered only minor disfiguring scars. We couldn't even get a lifelong-embarrassment factor into that case, what with plastic surgery and so forth."

"Another loss," said Palmer.

"What about the planes? Planes are always good," said Schwartz. "We've done well with our planes. It's our basic. And don't tell me we're dealing with babies or laborers in first-class cabins. Those are usually the first ones to go. We've had industrialists in those cabins. We've had good litigation."

"The problem with a plane," said Palmer, annoyed that Schwartz was missing the obvious, "is that you get one plane at most from any provable negligence. When you're dealing with aircraft and airlines, whenever a flaw is discovered, it's changed. Engines are always being redesigned. So are tails and wings, and anything that might remotely cause an accident."

Nathan Palmer rose in trembling indignation. "The terrible fact is that if you prove a flaw in one kind of airplane, that's the safest kind to fly next because they always fix it. We've never gotten more than one suit from any plane disaster. Not one."

"The cars were good," said Schwartz.

"Cars are another thing. But how many manufacturers would now consider mounting the gas tank in the rear bumper?" asked Palmer.

"The gas tank in the bumper was the best. Went up like bombs. We had hundreds of bombs on American highways and the best part of it was some idiot at the auto company had figured out it was cheaper to pay a judgment than to take the gas tank out of the bumper," said Rizzuto.

"We did do well on the gas tanks in the bumpers," sighed Schwartz.

"We made them change that policy," said Rizzuto.

"Fifteen years ago," said Schwartz. "What have we had since? Break-even airplanes, construction-company losses, and baby bottles that were at best a nuisance value to the company."

"If we could do surgeons, those big-income guys who do the fancy operations, then we would have something," said Schwartz.

"What would we get? Three surgeons at most? And what would we have to pay for it? The problem, gentlemen, is that paying for these accidents is breaking us."

"Makes you want to go back to honest law," said Schwartz.

"No such thing," said Rizzuto. "You remember what they taught us at law school? There are two things in law. Winning and losing."

"Yes, but what about the ethics they taught?" asked Schwartz. He had a problem he shared with the others. They hated to lose arguments even if winning got them nowhere. Perhaps that was why they had all entered law, Schwartz had often thought. It was competitive. There were winners and there were losers and when one applied his mind day in and day out to the angles of winning, other considerations tended to dissolve.

Like ethics. All three felt they had all the legal ethics they needed. They had studied enough to pass the California bar, and after that there was no need to follow their oaths. If they got into any trouble with an ethics committee, they could always bring it to court and probably win.

Besides, the way they operated, no one ever found out what they did. That was the genius of their method or, as Palmer had once said, the method of their genius.

"Our problem is we have been using our genius the wrong way," said Palmer.

"He's never gotten us into a bit of trouble," said Schwartz.

"That's because he knows how everything works," said Rizzuto.

"I have called you here today to tell you that if we continue to use our genius in the manner we have been, we will all be bankrupt within a year."

"God help us," said Schwartz.

"My bookie is going to carve my liver," said Rizzuto.

"I've got seven ex-wives, and I'm getting married again," said Palmer.

"Really? Congratulations. What's she like?" asked Rizzuto. He liked Palmer's taste in wives. He had made love to half of them, give or take. Which meant he'd come out even on his bets with himself. The gambling on which ones would and which wouldn't had been the best part.

"Like the other seven, of course," said Palmer.

"Nice," said Rizzuto, who thought it proper to wait until after the wedding before asking when Palmer would be taking another business trip.

"All of which is neither here nor there," said Palmer. "None of us is going to be able to support our human failings unless we change our ways."

"What failings?" asked Rizzuto. "I had a half-million dollars' worth of action going, and it was going to turn. It had to turn. You called me away. You cost me a half-million cool ones."

"I hardly consider a stock market that reacts in peculiar fashion a failing of my mathematical formulas."

"Yes," said Palmer, the most realistic of the three. "And I have at last found my own true love in number eight."

"Okay. You win. What are we going to do?" asked Rizzuto.

"You must have a plan of some sort," Schwartz said. "You never do anything you don't know the outcome of, unless it's marriage. Of course, you do know the outcome of that, don't you?"

"Don't be nasty, Arnold," said Palmer. He walked to the window, paused as the California sunlight bathed his fine features, turned to his partners as though addressing a jury, and then showed the other two, who basically found him a pain in the ass, why he was a worthy partner.

"I am thinking of a city. A city with doctors, lawyers, a mayor. A city with homes, with families. With mothers bringing up children, fathers supporting families. I am thinking of homes, entire family units. Industries. Their lives cut short by some deliberate negligence by a multinational corporation whose assets we can seize."

"I like it," said Schwartz. "A city has bankers and industrialists in it too."

"A city has hope. A city is a world unto itself. A city represents us all, everything that is most civilized about any culture. All our artists and great ideas come from our cities," said Rizzuto.

"Snuffed out cruelly," said Palmer.

"By a multinational whose assets we can freeze," said Schwartz.

They all nodded to the old scratched wood desk in the glass case.

"Well," said Palmer quite pleased with himself. "It looks as though we won't have to break out that one for a while, will we?"

"A city will be expensive for the genius," said Schwartz.

"Everything is expensive for the genius," said Palmer. "That's why we're in so much overhead trouble."

"But a city is going to be worth it," said Rizzuto, knowing he himself would now get back into action. With an entire city injured and in pain, he could create an image of the end of the world, which meant of course the end of a juror's world. The rewards would be enormous.

Thus it was decided in the elegant Century Park City offices in Los Angeles that a call be put in to the genius.

The price tag was a whopping five million dollars. When Palmer, Rizzuto & Schwartz agreed to deliver it immediately, there was one question.

"Do you have any particular city in mind?"

"No. Any one you think is right."

"I don't do things that aren't right," said the voice.

The phone call from the partners' office was picked up by an automatic program on CURE computers. While ordinarily sounds would be translated into written words, examined, and compared to a data base of flash signals to warn Smith of special dangers

needing his attention, this phone call from Palmer,
Rizzuto & Schwartz did not register as being received at any registered location. Someone had by-
passed the general electronic circuitry of the phone
company, something CURE's computers continued to
insist was not happening even while it was being done.

Nor did the computers pick up the word "Gupta"
coming back to Palmer, Rizzuto & Schwartz. There
was some indication of trouble because one of the
secretaries dutifully reported the preparation of a
disaster team. This was not only filed in the law
firm's computers but also secretly was forwarded to
the CURE data bank, which could not place its importance immediately.

In the city of Gupta, India, dawn came as it had
for aeons over the sacred mountains of Kalil, the sun
representing one of the million Hindu gods, shining
blood-red through the haze of morning.

From the first days of man-made fires, Gupta had
always been hazy. The dung used for fuel burned in
acrid smoky clouds, hardly lifted by passing breezes,
for Gupta was at the bottom of a bowl-shaped valley
ringed by mountains. He who controlled the mountains controlled Gupta. Warrior princes had ruled
here. Mogul invaders had ruled here. The British
had ruled here, and now the remnants of all their
seeds calling themselves Indians ruled here, Muslim
and Hindu and Sikh and Christian.

No one noticed the great death come upon them
because it walked surely like one who knew how
Gupta worked. It came first to the wife of a government official. It came with the hiss of jealousy.

How much more important she would be if her
husband was recognized as a true Indian in the cen-

tral government. But alas, in Gupta the colonialists still ruled.

She did not know where the voice came from. She knew it was somewhere and that if it were some intruder in her courtyard her husband would have him beaten.

"There are no colonialists here. India is free."

"Then what is that International Carborundum & Phospate factory doing here?"

"The people love it. It gives work. It gives high positions. It employs engineers and laborers. It makes us industrialized."

"It makes your husband, I am sorry to say, less respected in Delhi."

"You are a liar. You will be beaten. You will have your tongue cut in a thousand places."

The voice seemed to be coming from the walls. It was an American voice. International Carborundum & Phospate was American. Were they playing some trick? She turned so quickly she almost got tangled in her peach-colored sari. Was a god talking to her? Did she fail to make the proper sacrifices? Was her home made unclean by some act during a wrong time of her menstrual cycle? There were so many things this voice could be, but the last thing it could be was what it said it was.

"I am your friend, good woman. Look at all the major government ministers. Is there another who in his own domain has so many whites in high positions?"

"Oh, voice, you spread lies. And if you had a body it would die with a thousand cuts. If you had eyes they would be punctured. My husband is a regional administrator. Even the police chief bows to him."

"But, good woman, your husband does not have a major post in Delhi. Your husband does not sit in council with the ministers. Your husband follows orders and is kept at a distance like an untouchable."

"I will not listen to another word," said the woman. She clasped her hands to her ears and left the room. But in a few minutes she was back.

"Do not be insulting, voice, and I will listen to you. What is wrong at International Carborundum & Phosphate? Not that my husband is at fault."

"The Americans do not respect you. Certainly there are important jobs Indians have with the company, but not the crucial ones."

"An Indian is president of the Gupta installation," she answered. She had even seen his office, so large. So important, with so many wooden cabinets. It looked out over the fifteen-acre chemical plant like a tower of a Mogul prince. It was as modern, she was told when on tour of the factory, as any in America. She saw many impressive buttons and dials in many rooms.

The president of the local installation, a Brahman who had graduated from a British engineering school, had personally greeted all the wives of the important ministers.

"What are those wonderful buttons and dials?" asked one of the wives. "What magic do they perform?"

"I know what every one of them does," the president answered sharply.

"What does the shiny one with the light do?" asked the woman.

"It keeps nosy women in their place," he said, and laughed at his own joke. She bowed to the rebuke. But later it was revealed that one should never ask the president how any of the complicated controls and gauges worked. He knew exactly what he had to

know: that there were always Americans to take care
of everything. He was not to be bothered with the
petty tasks, but dealt with the higher concepts. He
sat behind a big desk and ordered people about. If
ever he wanted to know how any dial or button
worked, he would call in an American and order him
to explain.

But why should he ask? Did he ask the untouchables how they collected dung for the fires that burned
throughout the Gupta valley? This the woman remembered as the invisible voice spoke to her, and
the invisible voice began to make sense.

"The Americans are smarter than the British. The
British sat on horses, parading in fine uniforms, and
let others do the work. But the Americans know those
are not the people who run things. The people who
run things know how they work. And look at the
American factory in Gupta. Look at the jobs Indians
have. They sit at desks and collect money and they
are happy. But they do not know how to run the
factory. And the moment the Americans leave, all
they will have will be their fancy desks and fancy
offices and nothing and no one to order about. Do
you think the important ministers in Delhi do not
know this?"

"But my husband is blameless," pleaded the woman.

"Your husband is regional director. He is most to
be blamed."

"What can we do?"

"You can begin by insisting that Indians hold crucial, not ceremonial, posts."

"What is a crucial post?"

"Safety engineer."

"That is crucial?"

"That is most crucial. If the safety engineer does

not do his job, no one will be safe. If the president of
the factory does not show up for a week, who even
notices he is gone?"

"What if my husband beats me for my insolence?"

"He most certainly will beat you, but then he will
do what you told him."

"You know my husband."

"I know how things work."

In the offices of the English-language *Times* of
Gupta, a voice spoke to an editorial writer. The voice
sounded like it was coming from outside his window.
It sounded American.

"What you want Indians for is to let them sit
around and pretend they run things. Now, we're
lucky. We give them these phony jobs, call them
'president' and such. That's fine. Paying them sala-
ries is just another form of local bribe. We can accept
that cost. But heaven help us if one of these brown
bastards ever insists on being safety engineer."

"How do you keep them from it?"

"Simple. We make them believe the crucial jobs
are some form of janitorial work. Safety engineer is
close to maintenance engineer, which is another word
for broom-pusher. That's untouchable work to these
buggers."

"You mean they're the laughingstock of the home
offices of International Carborundum & Phosphate?"
said the writer.

"Shhh. Not so loud. We're near a newspaper."

The editorial writer looked out the window to see
which American was ridiculing his race. But outside,
he saw nothing but the rotting garbage of the streets
and a cow lazily strolling along with an untouchable
running behind waiting for fuel for the countless fires
that laid an eternal haze over Gupta.

And so, in a seemingly spontaneous eruption, the leaders of Gupta rose to demand that the American company employ Indians for what they called the most important jobs. The regional director led the demands but he had support from the local newspaper, whose banner editorial read: "WHAT FOOLS DO THEY TAKE US FOR?"

Since no one wanted to be a fool, a raging storm engulfed the home office of International Carborundum & Phosphate in Dover, Delaware, offices far less plush than those in Gupta, India.

"What the hell do they want to be safety engineers for? What the hell do they want to be maintenance engineers for? We couldn't give those jobs away there two years ago."

"Better give in to them, chief. Where else can we manufacture Cyclod B?" said the subordinate. Cyclod B was the main active ingredient of the insecticide Goodbye Bug. It sold enormously well in America in its attractive lemon-yellow can with a cartoon bug happily keeling over dead and being swept up by a dustpan and broom. Combined with other chemicals, Cyclod B killed bugs very effectively and made the countryside only moderately toxic. But alone, uncombined in formula, it contained two of the deadliest gases known to man, one of them a derivative of a now-outlawed World War I warfare agent.

International Carborundum had looked around the world for a place to manufacture Cyclod B. After announcing that a local resident would be president of the facility and that it would provide not only five thousand low-paying jobs but also a hundred important positions, the company found that it had its choice of the subcontinent. It chose Gupta because it was near a good railhead. It was far enough away from Delhi so that central-government officials would have to be bribed only occasionally, and it had a mixed Indian population so that the Hindus would not accuse International Carborundum & Phosphate of favoring Sikhs or Muslims or Christians—and vice versa for all the combinations that existed.

They could spread the wealth.

The decision from headquarters in Dover was an immediate yes. But with one warning.

"Make sure as hell they know how damned dangerous Cyclod B is."

"Bit difficult. We sort of sold the Indian government on the idea that Cyclod B is no more dangerous than water when properly used."

"How the hell did we do that?"

"We spread rupees around like manure."

"Just make sure we have good men in safety and maintenance."

Apparently someone knew how International Carborundum worked because the good men that were hired all had the best recommendations and degrees. And men with degrees did not like to go around turning valves and knobs like untouchables. The first thing they did was order new offices, with pretty secretaries, expensive desks, and many telephones, and then they assigned the task of monitoring to underlings. These underlings ordered smaller offices for themselves and shared secretaries, but each had a personal phone. They too hired subordinates for the menial work of reading meters and checking valves.

The safety-engineering budget increased fifteenfold within a week, and thereafter it took a full day and a half with stacks of paperwork requiring six or seven signatures to get so much as a mop delivered to a hallway.

Valves that had to be checked and lubricated every day now rarely saw a human hand. And in Gupta, a lone voice was heard. An American engineer mentioned to a local newspaper that the plant was being run dangerously, but the story was not printed because it smacked of American racism.

The man tried to explain that it was not the color of the man's skin monitoring the safety valves, but the monitoring itself. He even left a pamphlet for the newspaper editorial writer showing the dangers of Cyclod B.

"I will not even look at anything brought to me by a racist," said the editorial writer.

"I'll tell you what, you just keep it around. If you still have it in a week and you haven't used it, I'll buy it back for a hundred dollars American. But I think you'll need it."

"A racist attitude. We are not only safe, but perhaps even safer because these are the lives of our own people."

The man laughed at the editorial writer.

"The only reason International Carborundum & Phosphate manufactures Cyclod B here is that they wouldn't dare manufacture it in America or Europe. Now who are the racists?"

"You, sir, get out," said the editorial writer, who was deeply bothered by the man's voice. He could have sworn he had heard it before, but had never seen the face before. However, even if the man were a racist, he was a help. He took a safety pin and fixed a typewriter that had been sticking for years and was thought to be too badly damaged to be repaired.

"How did you do that?"

"I know how things work," said the man. He did not leave his name or explain why he had such hostility toward Indians running American factories.

It was not long before one of the gauges on the safety valves began flicking ominously toward the red zone, the danger area for the flow of Cyclod B. The only way to make sure the chemical was safe was to be sure it always stayed liquid, and that meant keeping it at a temperature below a certain level. In the hot valley, Cyclod B had to be constantly refrigerated.

It was morning when the lowest assistant noticed the dial edging dangerously close to the red zone, which meant the temperatures were rising in the holding tanks. He ran to the third assistant safety engineer with the warning. The third assistant knew this was very important and therefore was very careful in preparing his memorandum for the second assistant safety engineer.

It was so important he rewrote it four times to make sure his syntax was correct. Then he berated the secretary for the one spelling error. He would not allow strikeovers.

The second assistant safety engineer insisted his name be included in the memorandum three times instead of just once. The third assistant had his name mentioned enough, the second assistant pointed out, because he was the sender.

And so by the time the memorandum reached the main office of the safety-engineering department, the gauges were well into the red zone and the untouchable who was assigned to read them had taken his family out of the city. He knew what they meant. He had worked in the factory a long time and the American racists were the only ones who talked to him, and they explained things to him.

They had told him that when the needles on the temperature gauges hit red, he should do one of two things. The first was to run.

And what was the second?

"Place your head carefully between your legs, bend over very far, and kiss your ass good-bye."

Cyclod B became a gas quietly as the temperatures rose, and as it became gas it put pressure on the entire tank system, and as this happened other gauges began to creep into the danger zone, and as that happened, the director of safety engineering was meeting with his subordinates preparing their plan to increase the size of their department.

This memo read that there never could be too high a price for safety. It warned of the danger of chemicals. It proposed a most reasonable solution to the pressing personnel problem. More secretaries. Pretty ones, possibly from Bombay or Calcutta.

The pressurized gas burst one seam and that was all that was needed. It came out in a small grayish-white cloud, somewhat thicker than the normal haze of the Gupta valley.

The first person who smelled it was an untouchable gathering dung on the road. It smelled like a charcoal fire. He wondered who was burning expensive wood. The odor was somewhat pleasant and it tickled his nostrils. Then he realized there was no more tickling. His nostrils were numb, and his limbs were numb, and the sun had gone out of the sky.

He dropped just as the cow down the road had dropped. Silently the gray cloud spread slowly across the valley without any wind to disperse it. The cloud grew and moved through the factory and into the city, cutting down people more thoroughly and viciously than any Mogul invader.

Babies cried and then stopped crying as desperate mothers shook them and then fell themselves, dropping their children into the dust as they died. Mothers, even in death, were seen crouched over the bodies of their children as if to protect them.

The rich important people who were not in the factory area escaped by car. It was four days before the city was safe to enter. Everywhere was carnage. Indian Army soldiers had to wear gas masks, not as protection from the Cyclod B that had by now been slowly dissolved into the air, but to block the stench of rotting flesh.

At first, government officials, not wanting to lose a valuable factory, tried to run a logical inquiry. But an outcry arose from the survivors.

The *Times* of Gupta had proof that Cyclod B was a liquid so dangerous that International Carborundum & Phosphate would not dare manufacture it in an American or European country. They had instead carelessly chosen a valley in India whose heat could turn the liquid into a deadly gas.

A cry rang out for retribution. It was joined immediately by a firm of American lawyers, who announced to the world:

"What is the cost of a city? What is the cost of a civilization? The price to be paid must be so prohibitive that a Gupta can never happen again." These words came from Genaro Rizzuto himself just after he met with the Indian prime minister. Gupta had become a word synonymous with disaster.

Rizzuto even had a bumper sticker that read: "NO MORE GUPTAS."

The prime minister declined to have it put on the state limousine.

4

The first reports of the death of fifteen thousand people in India made little impression on the American media. It was just another third-world disaster, appearing in newspapers as a one-paragraph filler item. But when word came that an American factory was responsible, Gupta was a major story.

It was like Africa. A hundred thousand black Africans could be slaughtered by other blacks, and it would make little impact as a news story. Perhaps one or two mentions here or there. But if twenty black people were killed by white South African police, then it became a front-page story.

If Syria chose to kill twenty thousand of its citizens, wiping out its town of Hama, that might be mentioned or not. But if Israel was standing nearby while Arabs killed three hundred or so other Arabs at Sabra and Shatilla in Lebanon, that was front-page news. When the Israelis pulled out and the Arabs went back to killing each other in the same places, the news retreated to the inside pages.

Thus, when there was a white or European angle to a story, a filler item became a front-page disaster. International Carborundum & Phosphate was American. If an American factory had killed fifteen thousand people in Gupta, it was news.

Remo and Chiun heard the news while Remo was avoiding a movie camera in a Los Angeles studio. He had agreed to accompany Chiun to Hollywood as part of a vacation because Chiun, like Smith, thought Remo needed a rest. Both of them thought Remo was crazy. He thought they were crazy. The compromise was that Remo would go out to the West Coast with Chiun. Chiun would be allowed to secure whatever deal he thought he had going with a movie company, provided he did not appear before a movie camera. Remo would make sure Chiun didn't get himself in front of the cameras.

This was of course an impossibility, as Remo told Smith, because no one stopped Chiun from doing anything, and the most likely time for Chiun to do exactly what he wanted was when he had promised to fulfill someone else's wishes.

So Remo got word of the Gupta disaster at precisely the moment when Chiun was most likely to get himself seen. The cameras were rolling and Chiun, who just happened to be in his pure gold kimono with the ruby-encrusted red dragons, stepped forward to offer his humble assistance. Remo's buzzer rang. Smith had asked him to carry it. Smith had been watching a dangerous situation and had promised not to use Remo if he didn't have to. But if he had to, the buzzer would ring.

It rang just as Chiun stepped forward into the lights begging everyone's pardon, saying he did not wish to interfere and certainly did not wish to disturb anyone.

"But there is something of interest here that might be helpful to such wonderful stars as yourselves."

Remo took the buzzer device to the nearest pay telephone. He was supposed to dial the operator and then press the buzzer into the telephone receiver. This would automatically encode an access number directly to Smith.

Remo had been given access codes before but he had trouble getting them right. The numbers had to be more than seven digits lest unauthorized people accidentally dial into the most sensitive telephone lines in the nation. The more Remo became attuned to the mystical nature of the universe, the less he was able to deal with mechanical things.

So Smith had engineers devise a beeper device that even chimpanzees had been able to use after brief training with banana rewards. The absolute fail-safe, most user-friendly thing since the human kiss, it was called.

Remo got it right on the third try.

"What do you want, Smitty? Better hurry."

"There's a little problem in Gupta, India. I need to talk to you."

"What's important about Gupta, India?"

"What's happening at a Los Angeles law firm is important."

"That seems just as unimportant. Hey, I got to get back inside. Or do you want Chiun starring in some movie around the world?"

"I'm coming out there, Remo. This is important."

"Everything's important except American families, Smitty. Good-bye," said Remo. He moved quickly through the studio offices and onto the set. Chiun had made an arrangement with the producer to provide technical assistance. This producer was famous for action films and was doing a movie on a man with extraordinary powers. Chiun had corresponded with

him, saying he knew how people could naturally do
wondrous things, without props or tricks.

When the producer had asked what things, Chiun
answered: anything the producer wanted. What Smith
did not know, and Remo understood most well, was
that Chiun's main ambition was to get credit for all
the secret work he and Remo had done.

Chiun had never understood, or wanted to understand, that America was not some feudal kingdom
employing assassins to make or unmake emperors,
but a democracy that was run by rules.

Secrecy for Chiun was sneaking up on someone,
not keeping your mouth closed after you had been
successful at it.

His great ambition, having had the histories of
Sinanju turned down by every publishing house in
New York, was to have a movie made of them. There
was no chance this would happen. These histories,
records of each Master of Sinanju, went on for forty-
two thousand pages and Chiun would not allow one
word to be cut. If made into a movie, the histories of
Sinanju would have run twenty-four hours a day for
months.

A wily producer, hearing of free technical assistance, had given a Hollywood promise to look at part
of the histories, promising that if they could cut the
running time to six weeks they might have something there, but of course it would have to be in
English. Chiun had said the histories lost something
in English, but he agreed to go out to the Coast to
discuss it. Now as Remo got to the set he saw Chiun
showing one of the actors how to throw his arm
powerfully enough to actually make a car shake. Everyone was exicted. Everyone was applauding. The
director thought this was magnificent. But somehow,

and none of the movie people knew how, Chiun had
to be very near the star to make the trick work.

"Could the technical help possibly wear a less
glaring kimono? That gold and red just sucks up the
attention of the entire screen," called out the director.

"Oh, this little thing?" asked Chiun, touching a
long fingernail to the gold embroidery.

"Yeah. Red and gold. It's like a traffic light and
makes the heroine look like a sidewalk, sir. Could
you change it?"

"I am afraid I have nothing else," said Chiun
humbly.

Remo knew there were fourteen steamer trunks of
his kimonos back at the hotel.

"Can we drop a gray robe over him or something?
My light readings are going through the ceiling,"
said the cameraman.

"Does he really have to be on the set?" asked the
assistant director.

Chiun nodded yes, with apologies. He said he
gave the actor a sense of confidence by being nearby.

Could Chiun be nearby out of camera range, then?

"I will try, O great artists of the West, whose glory
inspires a thousand poets, whose beauty shames the
blossoms of the dawn."

"Okay, a gray cloth, and let him stand three paces
back and we have it," said the director.

Someone called "Action" and the hero reached
out, trying to push the car. Chiun, being helpful,
moved in somewhat closer, and with abject apologies
found that his gray covering was coming off.

The scene was reshot forty-two times and each of
those times the Master of Sinanju just couldn't quite
keep the gray cover on, nor could anyone make it
stay on. And when the rushes were viewed that

evening, the only thing visible was Chiun smiling at the camera as the car shook, while the hero remained almost invisible as the gray cloth covered his head.

Back at the hotel, Remo waited with Chiun for Smith's call. They had often met in hotel rooms, but one right in Beverly Hills, Smith felt, would attract too much attention.

"Do you think Smith will want screen credit?" Chiun wondered. "He is our legal employer."

"I don't think he'll mind not being mentioned," said Remo.

"Yes. He is crazy, but then again, your entire race is crazy," said Chiun. And now, for the first time in years, Remo chose to answer him back. He did not choose to let it slide.

"No, you're crazy. You worry about the treasure of Sinanju. When it was stolen a few years ago, you dropped everything and went looking for it. But what did it do for thousands of years? It sat there and did nothing."

"It was there," said Chiun.

"So what?" said Remo. "You never spent a penny of it."

"It was there in case."

"In case what?"

"You know how we became assassins. The village starved. Babies had to be put into the waters because there was no food for them. The assassins made sure there was food and have been honored by the village ever since."

"What you earn in tribute in one week could feed them for the next century. And this idea of people respecting Sinanju, what do you care what they think?"

"You don't care?"

"I care what you think, little father. I do not care what some people I never met think. I care what I think about me. That's important."

Chiun thought a moment. He did not understand what Remo meant about thinking about himself. Chiun did not think much about himself. He had understood at a young age, so young he could not even remember, that he was wonderful. And if someone else did not think the same way, a horrible death was too good for him. What was there to think about?

He wondered if this was the madness of the willows spoken about in the Ming Dynasty. Royals would be found staring at willow branches, doing nothing else until servants brought them back to their palaces.

What was this thinking about oneself? Chiun could not fathom it. Did it have to do with judging oneself? Why, that could mean disliking oneself, and that of course was impossible. He smiled briefly and decided to watch Remo closely for the rest of the day.

Smith arrived at two A.M. and set up a meeting just outside the city limits in a car he had rented. Smith insisted Chiun be there. There were communications problems with the Master of Sinanju, and to be sure Smith had never quite understood what Chiun meant in some of his flowery language. But Chiun was a professional. And if there were questions about duties, an added weight of gold could always solve any moral dilemma. In fact, there were no moral dilemmas.

Remo, on the other hand, was a patriot. He had been evaluated carefully through psychological tests before he was even considered. And the truth was, a patriot was a lot more difficult at times to deal with than a cash-and-carry mercenary.

And there were special problems with Palmer,

Rizzuto & Schwartz, problems Smith wondered if either Remo or Chiun could handle.

When he saw the headlights come up the dirt road he blinked twice. The other car blinked back twice. Then three times. Then the headlights went off. Remo had broken the lights when he got the signals wrong. He drove the last hundred yards on a starless, moonless night as dark as the bottom of a mineshaft, at seventy miles an hour, without so much as grazing the shoulder of the narrow road.

Chiun and Remo got into Smith's rented car. They sat in the back, Chiun protesting that Smith deserved the place of honor and they as his loyal servants should sit up front as drivers.

This was in English. In Korean he noted that this meeting at an ungodly hour on a dirt road was another sign of Smith's mental aberrations and sooner or later "this lunatic will get us killed."

Smith did not understand Korean.

"And greetings to you, Chiun," said Smith. "We have a problem. I had hoped that Remo might get some needed rest. Frankly, and you both know this, I've been most worried about Remo's actions lately."

"Nobody has a gun to your head, Smitty. You don't have to use me," said Remo.

"Please don't be defensive. But as a matter of fact, someone does have a gun to my head. Someone has a gun to the head of all America. And that's why I'm here."

In Korean, Chiun wondered how someone could hold a gun to the head of a country, since Smith was always claiming America did not have an emperor. Did one put a pistol against the Rocky Mountains? Did one shoot at the Mississippi? Or was that the knee of the country and not the head? But to Smith

he commented gravely that a gun to a country's head
was a disaster not only for the country but for everyone living there.

He held his chin thoughtfully in his long fingernails and nodded, full of the gravity of the situation.

"I don't know if you are aware of it, Remo, but
America has become dangerously litigious."

"What is this 'litigious'?" asked Chiun.

"It means suing, Master of Sinanju. Americans are
using lawyers for every grievance, real or imagined.
The courts are clogged. But that's not the problem."

"Perhaps more assassinations and fewer lawsuits
would solve the problem. As you know, Emperor
Smith, each injustice dealt with by a head on a wall
not only solves the immediate problem but five others as the wrongdoers see justice done swiftly and
surely," said Chiun.

"No. No. That's just what we can't have. That's
just what America is not about, what we can't be
about. That's just why we're here, working secretly,
so that we'll have our laws to live by and still get
through these times of chaos," said Smith.

"Of course," said Chiun. "Your genius is simplicity
itself."

He glanced at Remo to see if Remo understood
what Smith was talking about. Remo was not smirk-
ing. He seemed to take it seriously.

"Excuse me, Emperor Smith, but your wisdom
has such power it envelops worlds too large for your
assassin. I would understand it better in Korean.
Would you be so kind as to allow Remo to explain it
to me?"

"Certainly," said Smith. "I think it would be helpful. Remo, explain it to him."

"He's not going to understand it. He doesn't want to understand it," said Remo.

"He expressed an interest, and I think the courteous thing to do is to accede to his request. I also think it might clear up some misunderstandings the Master has about this country," said Smith. "And make him even more effective than he is now."

Chiun blinked. He could not believe his ears. He routinely treated Smith as an exalted emperor, referring to himself sometimes as a humble assassin. But this attitude was not intended to be taken seriously. It was only to show that besides Chiun's awesome magnificence, he was also capable of being humble. In fact, because he was so perfect in all manner of things, his humility was to be appreciated as even greater. But Smith had said, in words out of his own mouth, and Chiun had understood every one of them, that Chiun could be more effective.

This meant there was something he did that might need improvement. The insult hit him like a steaming towel across the face. If he did not have perfect control of his breath he would have been aghast. Instead he waited to see if Remo would let that insult pass.

And pain of pains, Chiun witnessed in his own grief that Remo said nothing, except to explain the nonsense of the American Constitution.

"So what we do secretly, and why we do things secretly, is to support the belief that a nation can run by laws. And what we do is make sure it survives in those little extralegal ways it needs in a dangerous world," said Remo in Korean, knowing Chiun could never grasp the idea of a constitution because he believed that all governments were run by power and threat, and therefore needed assassins. If America were different, why then did it need the services of the grandest line of assassins of all time, the House of Sinanju?

But Remo was not prepared for Chiun's enraged response.

"How dare you talk to me of that drivel, when the one who has given you all you know, all you hold that makes you what you are, has been vilified in your presence?"

"I didn't hear it. What did Smith say? Did I miss something?"

"Did you miss something?" squeaked Chiun. He could not even bear to look at Remo anymore.

"Yeah. What did I miss? What's wrong?" asked Remo.

"What is wrong? What is wrong?" asked Chiun, his voice rising to a squeaky crescendo.

Smith did not understand their Korean dialect. He had tried to study Korean once just to find out what the two were saying in his presence, but he discovered that many of the terms used in Sinanju were not in a Korean dictionary because they were so archaic. It was as if a time capsule had captured a language four thousand, five hundred years old and had kept it pure.

Still, even though he did not understand what they were talking about, it seemed to him that they were being a bit too emotional for a discussion about the Constitution of the United States, especially since it was Smith's opinion that Chiun believed the Constitution was some form of American poem, like a religious chant that everyone said and did not really believe in.

"That's what I said. What is wrong?" Remo snarled.

"He asks what is wrong. Did you not hear the

venom from Smith's own lips? Did you hear what he said?"

"He was talking about the Constitution, which you don't think means anything to begin with."

"He said to a Master of Sinanju that a Master of Sinanju could be more effective. That is what he said."

"More effective in his context, protecting America through secrecy. Protecting the things of America that are valuable. Like the rights of people."

"What about the rights of a Master of Sinanju, respected lo these thousands of years in courts and palaces? Gloried from Samarkand to St. Petersburg. Honored by Ming and Claudian dynasties. What about the rights of the man you call 'little father,' the one you have just heard degraded with your own ears? Do these rights mean nothing?"

"You don't understand what Smith meant. He wasn't talking about your skills . . ."

"I understand. I understand that when you take insults and disrespect from a pupil, then you can expect it from the world. You have allowed me to be shamed in front of . . . of a white."

"You don't like it from any color, so why do you pick on white?"

"You're white. You're all white. You've always been white. You stick together, don't you?"

"Little father, I love you. But Smitty doesn't even understand enough to know he insulted you. Believe me. If he had, I would have spoken up. I would never let anyone insult you."

"Then let's work for a sane emperor. Or a tyrant. This is a rare time in history. Tyrants and kings are regaining their power. Look at Korea itself. Once thought lost to communism in the north, which proved to be only an ugly mask for a beautiful kingly dynasty transferred from father to son. Communism is on the rise all over. And that means tyrannies, if not kingships. This could well be the glory age of assassins. Let us leave this insulting churl with the face of a lemon."

"I love my country, too, little father," said Remo. "I'm sorry. I do. I just don't care about money."

"A wound to a father's heart."

"I'm sorry," said Remo. And the conversation over, Remo turned back to English and back to Smith.

"Well, that was a spirited discussion on our legal system, wasn't it?" said Smith.

"Yeah," said Remo. His voice felt hoarse, not because of the volume he had used but because of the emotion that had come upon him. He honestly did feel torn now between Sinanju and America. Once he thought he could make them work in harmony, each serving the other. Now he realized this was impossible. East was East. And West was West.

"Your Constitution rings with the beauty of your greatest poets, its words such harmony of the soul that flowers blush in shame," said Chiun. "Now I fully understand that wonderful document."

"Good, I think you do," said Smith. "I think he does in a deeper way than I might have imagined. Don't you think so, Remo?"

"Sure," said Remo curtly.

"Well, because we are a nation of laws, the legal system is crucial. As cumbersome and as difficult as it is, it is the one key protection we have from ourselves, from rapacious politicians and bureaucrats, from the powerful harming the weak, do you see?"

Remo stared out the window into the darkness. Chiun examined his hands. Smith continued.

"Because there are so many lawsuits nowadays, and because the judgments have become so high, costs of producing things have gone up. We're losing some of our finest surgeons because they refuse to pay the high insurance premiums. Obstetricians are so racked by lawsuits their malpractice insurance sometimes comes to three-quarters of their income; many are leaving the profession. Industries are being threatened with shutdown."

Smith paused. Remo said, "Un-huh," and then examined his nails. Chiun said just about the same thing but it came out as a laudation of Smith's wisdom. Then Chiun looked out the window.

"And we have found one particular law firm to be the biggest problem in this area. They have raised ambulance-chasing to a science. I'm sure they're behind many of the terrible tragedies they jump on, but we can't prove it."

"You want us to eliminate them?" said Remo.

"No. This is a legal problem. You can't go around killing lawyers. What we must do is remove them from within the system. We have to get legal proof to get them disbarred and thrown in jail. Once they are ruined it will act as an example to other ambulance chasers, or at least cut down the number of industry-threatening negligence cases."

"Just a minute. I know you have thousands of little gnomes everywhere, all of them feeding information into your computers without them knowing about it. Why can't you do it with that law firm?"

"We have," said Smith. "And everyone has died— not just died, but died in an accident. A shower suddenly spits out scalding water at a secretary with a heart problem. She dies. A junior lawyer working undercover for one of the government agencies has his roof collapse on him, killing him. Now, the roof suffered what appeared to be normal decay in the joists. And this shower had always lacked protection against spurts of extra-hot water. So we can't prove a thing."

"So?" said Remo.

"So we want people to gather evidence who can't be killed by accidents."

"I can be killed by an accident," said Remo.

"Theoretically, I suppose, yes," said Smith.

"It's not a theoretical life, Smitty."

In Korean, Chiun said, "Charge him a higher price and say yes. It is all the same nonsense when you are working for a lunatic."

"All right. Where do we begin?" said Remo in English.

"There's been an accident in Gupta, India. We're sure Palmer, Rizzuto & Schwartz are behind it. Go there. See if you can figure out how they did it, and see if you can link it to those shysters. Rizzuto was on hand a little bit too early and seems to have the ear of the prime minister."

"India?" said Chiun. "Ah, the Moguls. The grandeur of the rajahs. India has always been a second home to the House of Sinanju."

"Be careful, Remo," said Smith. "We don't know how these guys work. They even have programs that seem to foil our computers. They can conduct conversations we can't break into. And they seem to be able to cause accidents at will. They can make anything not work."

"So can I," said Remo.

"On purpose," said Smith.

He wondered why there was a sudden change of activity. He was good at wondering. But when he wondered, it was different from others, and it always had been. He wondered what he would find when he saw something that was not working properly.

It did not have to be a big thing. It just was very clear to him, clearer than sunshine. He could not remember when things like clocks and faucets were not obvious in their workings.

And so when he tinkered with the program systems of Palmer, Rizzuto & Schwartz, the thing that stuck him this day was that an element of surveillance had changed.

First, there was the increased activity in the data base of Palmer, Rizzuto & Schwartz. That meant at one time someone was doing something to the Palmer, Rizzuto & Schwartz information that he, or she, shouldn't have been doing. This had led to a simple refraction program based on binary algorithms that spit out the names of the perpetrators as easily as if it were a list of clients.

There were four so far, including a secretary and a young lawyer.

But what was apparent most of all in these strange intrusions into the sanctity of Palmer, Rizzuto & Schwartz was the hint of a larger system.

It was as obvious as a leaky faucet. Someone meant Palmer, Rizzuto & Schwartz no good and was watching them. And when this system, so organized and relentless, suddenly downgraded its attempt to rifle information from the law firm's computers, this man who knew how things worked understood there was a different, more subtle attack coming against the people who had made him so wealthy.

He phoned Palmer at his home even though it was Palmer's wedding night.

Palmer's wife answered, screaming.

"You can speak to that bastard anytime. I'm leaving," she said.

"Hello, Nathan," he said. "It's me."

"I can't afford any more help. We haven't made anything on Gupta yet."

"I've called with a warning."

"How much?"

"No charge this time. I was just tinkering. You know how I love to tinker."

"What's the warning?"

"You're going to come under attack from a new direction."

"Well, that's a relief. I wasn't trusting anyone there for a while."

"I am afraid this one is going to be more dangerous than the others. You see, from what I can tell just by understanding the programs they used to get at your confidential information, this is not the kind of organization to pull back. If it appears to be pulling back, it's only bringing in something far more dangerous."

"We don't have money yet. Can you handle it?"

"Of course. I understand how everything works."

5

As Remo and Chiun descended the ramp from the jet, Chiun breathed deeply and sighed.

"Our second home. Sinanju has done some of its finest work here. The great pearl of Hortab was earned here, by the Master Chee, in a very delicate and beautiful assassination. It seems—"

Remo inhaled and spit.

The airport, like most of India, smelled of animal and human waste. The massive country made for beautiful pictures and awful odors. Like most of civilization for most of history it had yet to solve its sewage problems. Raw human waste ran in the streets. Garbage was rarely collected in the lower-class neighborhoods, and in the rich neighborhoods it was the prime pickings of gangs. The life of a sacred cow was more important than the life of most citizens and the great holy river of the Ganges, had it run through any Western country, would have been called a pollution danger of immense proportions. Instead the Indians defecated in it, urinated in it, threw their garbage in it, and then bathed in it.

"Son," said Chiun. "I will show you India as you

have never seen it. It will be your second home also."

"I'd prefer an armpit," said Remo.

"It is because you do not know how to travel. Before we do anything we must pay our respects to the reigning emperor, and we must go properly," said Chiun.

"They have a president too," said Remo. "You'll find it the same system as America, which you don't understand."

"Really? If it is the same system as America, then why does the son succeed the mother? That is how you tell a throne. Not by whether people think they vote or not. Dynasties are matters of succession."

"Yeah. He's not going to meet you. India doesn't have kings or emperors or rajahs anymore. That's backward. They're not that backward anymore. They're going to laugh at us."

Chiun ignored the remarks and hired bearers for a litter roofed with a saffron parasol. He hired trumpeters and callers to announce his coming. And then, with his fourteen steamer trunks ornamented in gold and red ribbons, he set about the return of a Master of Sinanju to the palaces of India. When his bearers brought him to the gates of the presidential palace in Delhi, the horns were told to sound arrival and a bard was instructed to sing, in Hindi, praises to Sinanju, the House of Sinanju, the Masters of Sinanju, and all that was Sinanju.

"They're going to laugh us out of here, little father," said Remo. "That is, if they don't start shooting." The former prime minister had just been shot by her own Sikh bodyguards and now her son was prime minister, and he was supposed to be surrounded by heavily armed Hindus, some of them his rela-

tives. These soldiers were less professional than the
Sikhs that had turned on his mother, and there were
rumors that passersby had been shot by excitable
guards just for making too much noise. But in Delhi,
with so many dead normally on the streets, no one
could really tell the difference. As a commentator
had once said, a human life in India had all the worth
of a toilet-paper wrapper in America. Remo waited
in the litter, chuckling. Chiun waited beside him,
the soft warm breezes blowing his wisps of white hair
like pennants.

Finally the gates opened and Remo's jaw dropped.

The prime minister was standing there, his hands
clasped in front of him in formal Hindu greeting.

"We have heard of your arrival, O Master of
Sinanju. Let India be home to Sinanju and all its
glory," said the prime minister.

Remo couldn't believe his ears. He knew this man
was an engineer and had graduated from a modern
British university. Yet here he was paying homage to
a house of assassins. Remo had learned the stories of
the Masters, but he had never quite believed the
historical part where this Master or that had saved
this pharaoh or that king. Or that they were publicly
glorified.

He believed in Sinanju, the doing of it, but not
the trappings. And here were the trappings come to
life.

Chiun sat pleased as punch. He did not bother to
say he told Remo so. That would come later. Instead
he answered the prime minister.

"We are glad to be home among our friends," he
said. "It has become known to us that your mother
has met with a tragedy. While we share your grief,
we cannot help but think that your mother might

still be with us if you had employed Sinanju instead of Sikh guards."

"Master of Sinanju," said the Prime Minister of India. "We always have a place for you in our service."

Chiun raised a hand. His gray traveling robe fluttered in the breeze.

"Would you repeat that for my son?" asked Chiun.

"Consider yourself hired," said the prime minister. "Everyone of importance in India appreciates the virtues of Sinanju. You are, of course, a legend."

"Would you, Remo, explain what we are doing in America?" said Chiun. "Listen to the nonsense to which Sinanju has been reduced, O leader of the great Indian peoples."

"No I wouldn't," said Remo. "We don't work for anyone. We're visitors."

"Then you are welcome and your employ is welcome also."

"We're busy. Thank you. Some other time," said Remo, and then whispered to Chiun:

"We're not supposed to let anyone know who we work for. You know that. Why'd you tell him to ask me?"

"Because I am too ashamed to say it myself. Look, this is how Sinanju should be treated. See? Can you imagine an American president coming to the gates of the White House and welcoming us? No. Instead we sneak around like thieves in the night, always afraid someone will hear us. This," said Chiun, pointing to the prime minister, "is where we belong."

"It stinks," said Remo.

"It's home," said Chiun.

"Stinks."

"Home."

"You are both welcome," said the prime minister.

"We've got business. We'd better be leaving," said Remo, and he nudged Chiun.

"Shortly we will be back and then your life will be as safe as your mother's should have been. We will sacrifice at the Ganges for her."

"And may a thousand gods bring good fortune to you, Master of Sinanju. And also to your son."

"Yeah, thanks," said Remo, nudging a litter bearer with his heel to speed their departure.

Chiun was outraged all the way to Gupta, a two-day journey by train. Remo had met a ruler who wished to employ Sinanju and all he could say was, "Yeah, thanks." Where was Remo's training? Had he forgotten the laudations already, the praises for a king or a duke or a prince or a pharaoh?

"Quite honestly, little father," said Remo, "I assumed the laudations for pharaohs were not something I was going to need right away."

"It's good to learn."

"Why?"

"Because it is proper training. The cloth is made of a thousand threads even if you don't see the crucial ones that hold the seams."

"What good does it do me to know the lower kingdom has to be mentioned before the upper kingdom and that my voice must rise on the first inflection in Thebes, or that only during a drought should I mention Luxor or Abu Simbel to a pharaoh?"

"Because it does," said Chiun. "You don't greet a friendly monarch with an American 'Yeah, thanks.' That's what you say to the lunatic Smith. Not to a real ruler who inherited a throne from his mother and may well give it to an heir, who just might have good work for the House of Sinanju."

This said, Chiun refused to talk further and was

silent through Patwar, Kanpur, Galior, Nagpur, Nizamabad, and Tirupati, until they reached the mountains that surrounded the valley of Gupta, where they saw the steep paths up to the mountain ridges.

They could smell the strange odors of Cyclod B still lingering in the air—not strong enough to be harmful, for only they could sense it. But it was there nevertheless, faint hints of a substance that could fatally damage a nervous system. Remo and Chiun used different breathing patterns to keep their pores open. But other travelers hardly noticed the odor. There was a convoy of medical workers and of course truckloads and truckloads of American cameramen.

A child was hit by a speeding army truck, and an American news team jumped out to interview him, while the mother tried to revive him.

But as soon as they found out America wasn't responsible, one of the cameramen called out, "Nothing here. A hundred thousand people die like this every week. Doesn't mean anything."

One of the newsmen wanted to interview Remo, but he dodged him. Chiun, seeing a camera, allowed himself to be spoken to.

He was here for a vacation, he said, to be among his good friends in Gupta.

"But most of them are dead," said the reporter.

"Whoever is left," said Chiun.

There was a strange silence in the city as the caravans made their way down into the bowl valley that housed the city of Gupta.

In one sector was a modern array of tanks and pipes that made up International Carborundum & Phosphate. They appeared still to be working. Remo felt Chiun touch his arm.

"Look," said Chiun. "Look."

"At what?"

"At everything. Has insolence also blinded your eyes? What do you see?"

"I see a city. I see mountains. I think the factory is still working. I don't know if it's still dangerous or what."

"You see and you don't see," said Chiun. "It was gas that killed. Look around you."

"These mountains make a bowl," said Remo.

"Now we are supposed to look for people who cause accidents, who make profit from them. If this is so, then they chose their site well. Whoever did this knows how to use the land. The gas would sit in the bowl a long time and not be blown away."

In the city, life was returning. The places of those who had died were taken by people from other cities who had no places. It occurred to Remo, seeing this, that the population explosion people criticized was really nature's way of keeping the race alive. Though thousands had died horribly, in time it would not even be remembered.

A young boy with large dark eyes and a big smile ran after Remo and Chiun's litter, begging and not getting anything, his smile turning into a frown and his happy chatter to curses. Remo laughed and gave the boy some change. Immediately scores of children poured from doorways and ran after the litter.

In their joy and laughter and in their numbers Remo felt that in India life was stronger than death. Chiun had never said this. He said there was an eternal balance between what the Masters called light and darkness, life and death, something and nothing.

Chiun also insisted on making proper sacrifices at five different temples to five different gods. At the temple of Shiva he suggested Remo make a personal sacrifice of a goat or a dove.

Remo, who had been raised in a Catholic orphanage in Newark, looked at the many-armed model of the god surrounded by symbolic flame, the "destroyer of worlds" as he was called, and just shook his head. He couldn't do it.

"He is special to you, Remo. All the prophecies about a dead man returning to become a Master of Sinanju involve Shiva, Remo," said Chiun.

"Yeah," said Remo. "I know." But he didn't go into the temple and he didn't make a sacrifice. He did not say a Hail Mary either. He just turned away and went back to the litter.

At the factory Remo was told he could not enter, but must wait in line.

"You cannot get work by pushing ahead and showing rudeness," said the official at the gate.

Remo looked back over the line.

"You mean all these people are waiting for work here?"

"Of course, these are good jobs."

"But I thought these were dangerous jobs. Deadly jobs."

"Don't you dare say that. We will never consider you."

From the litter Chiun berated the man for not showing more respect, and freely used the name of the prime minister. The gates opened and the guardian gave a small bow.

"This is civilization," said Chiun. "Where in America do you get proper courtesy?"

"You mean keeping hundreds waiting while we are shown deferential treatment?"

"Of course. You are against deferential treatment?"

"Yeah. Kind of. I kind of feel sorry for these people. I hate to see them ignored like that, just for us."

"Just for us?" asked Chiun with anger. "There is never just us. There is, most of all, most importantly, us. But I should not be surprised that you think of 'us' as a just, as nothing, something to be ignored and reviled. You are the one who does not care for money."

"Right. We don't need it. What do we need it for? You have all the robes you can ever wear. We get everything we ask for paid for by the organization, and that isn't much. It's a roof over our heads at most. So what else do we need?"

"Remo, do not make me sick," said Chiun.

At the Gupta plant of International Carborundum & Phosphate, Chiun freely bandied about the name of the prime minister and was accorded special respect. Seeing that he was shameless in his demands, the Indian employees, who respected shamelessness, gave him just about everything he wanted. While the American investigating engineers were delayed, dallied with, lied to, and fawned over to mislead them, Chiun and Remo got the real scoop.

"It was some stupid little valve that went. How should I know?" said the president of the local plant, Rashad Palul. He wore a lightweight English suit with an English school tie. He smoked English cigarettes and lit them with an English lighter. His English diction and grammar were impeccable. Remo felt like he was talking to some British lord.

"What do the American engineers say?"

"Something or other," said Rashad Palul. "They're dreadfully boring."

"I heard people weren't doing the proper maintenance."

"Rubbish. I increased the maintenance budget fiftyfold. You can't blame maintenance. I put the very best in charge of safety and increased the budget. Have you heard of the lawsuit?"

"I know some American lawyers are over here."

"By Jove, they certainly are. The sums they are demanding! Might put International Carborundum & Phosphate in a sticky position, what? Don't you think? Not that the Americans will get what they're after. They won't earn much here, the blighters."

"Why not?"

"Do you know the average worth of an Indian citizen? I'm not talking about us, you know, of course. I am talking about the commoners."

"No, I don't," said Remo, thinking about the smiling boy who had cadged money from him. It was only a grand accident, Remo had thought, that he had been born in America and that boy born here. Because if the opposite were true, Remo did not see how even he would be any different from the millions of Indians. There was just no way out for the common people here. That was the glory of America. That was what America meant to him. It was hope. That was what was lacking in a country like this. Who you were born was who you would be for the rest of your life.

"I would say on an average for a breadwinner, the award at most would be three hundred dollars. And that is high. That is a maximum price on his life."

"And for a boy?" asked Remo.

"No one's son? No one important?"

"A beggar," said Remo.

"Ten dollars. A dollar. A copper bowl. Whatever. They are of little importance. There are so many of them."

"There have to be with the way you dips run a country. India isn't run. It's excreted," said Remo.

"I beg your pardon," said Rashad Palul.

"My son, who is also a friend of the prime minister, sometimes has strange feelings about the oddest things," said Chiun. "Now, Palul, let us turn ourselves to important things. I do not care about the valves either."

"They're only the things that caused the damned disaster in the first place," muttered Remo. He looked out the windows at the mountains of Gupta, majestic peaks of strong beauty, each veined with trails leading down to the city.

"Who was responsible for the valves?"

"The entire department."

"Were there any new people in the department?"

"The entire department was new."

"And who was responsible before them?"

"An American engineer and some untouchables. You know how crazy Americans are. They did not see the difference between an untouchable and a Brahman as you do, sir."

"They are a peculiar race."

"The British understood the difference."

"The British understand these things," said Chiun. "Generally an intelligent people."

"Except for Henry the Eighth," said Remo, "who did his own killing and didn't pay Sinanju. Right?"

"Are you perchance from Sinanju, of the legendary Masters of Sinanju?" asked Palul.

"The very same," said Chiun, looking over to Remo to see if he noticed the proper respect being paid.

"Oh, gracious. No wonder you're friends of the P.M. By Jove, this is a most remarkable bit of good fortune. We must have you to dinner. Oh please, don't say no. You are our most honored guests."

"No," said Remo.

"He is affected by the sun," said Chiun.

"The House of Sinanju, you know, served a lord near here."

"Of course we know," said Chiun. "And so does he, when he studies his lessons."

"The House of Sinanju here in lowly Gupta . . ." said Palul.

"Are you listening to this good man, Remo?" asked Chiun.

Remo did not answer.

"He has emotional problems," Chiun confided to Palul.

"Get back to the valves. None of you guys from Nepal to Korea knows how a damned valve works. That's why you're all so damned backward," Remo said.

Chiun chuckled. "He is the worst with any equipment. He cannot dial a telephone without falling over his own fingers. Nothing works when he attempts to run it."

"Is he retarded?"

"Only in some areas," said Chiun.

"Back to business, please," said Remo. He thought about the little boy outside. The less everyone else cared about him, the more Remo felt sorry for him. He might not even make it to manhood, and no one would know. No one would care, and the rich would send their sons to school in the West to then make pronouncements about the disparity between north-south wealth and how it should be redistributed. All of these things said by the rich of those countries because the poor couldn't afford an education. None of these leaders of the poor countries would share so much as a crust of bread with their poor, and yet for some reason they expected other nations to do what they refused to do.

"What has changed here in the last year?" asked Chiun.

"If anything, safety and maintenance, which the American engineers blamed for the leakage, have been improved. Vastly. Our budget has grown in these areas."

"Good," said Chiun. "And how did that come about?"

"Well, there was a strong movement to replace the American engineer, to put Indians in that position. And we did. We put many in that position. We had three administrators to begin with."

"And who watched these valves?"

"I don't know. I don't bother with those things. I am president of this local branch, not some rag runner."

"Please be so kind as to tell me who is in charge of the valves."

"I don't know."

"Find out," said Chiun.

It took almost half a day to get the information, with one director after another coming in and out of the office and each of them thinking it was peculiar that someone so lofty as their president would care about some valve or other. They were all sure it was being taken care of by another department.

They all knew it used to be taken care of by some American engineer and a group of untouchables.

"How did the change happen?" asked Chiun.

"What do you care, little father? Let's go down and look at where it happened."

"It did not happen there," said Chiun. "How did the change happen?"

"It just happened. There was a spontaneous demand to put our own people in charge."

"Then nowhere was where it came from," said Chiun. And he asked from whom the president of the branch had first heard this spontaneous demand.

"It was all over," said Rashad Palul.

"No. Nowhere has to come from somewhere," said Chiun, and insisted that Palul question all his subordinates.

Some had read about it in the papers. Others had thought a local administrator was behind it. The editorial writer of the English-language *Times* of Gupta claimed it was his own idea.

"From my indignation at the arrogance of the racist West. From my firm rooting in third-world struggles. From my sense of being an Indian."

Remo grabbed him by his legs, pressed his foot to the man's throat which now was adjacent to the rug in the office of the factory president, and asked the editorial writer to clarify his statement.

"From voices. White-sounding voices. I overheard them saying insulting things."

"And where did these voices come from?"

"Outside my window."

"And who were they?"

"I did not see them. But they were your typical American racists looking down on everyone else. And they said the important thing not to let Indians have was the right to be in charge of important things. And that got my goat. Now will you please put me back on my feet?"

Remo yanked the man's heels upward, slapping

his head around on the carpet like a yo-yo, and then righted the man and set him firmly on his feet.

"You just can't go around doing that to people," said the editorial writer.

"I do it all the time," said Remo.

"These voices really got you doing, didn't they?" asked Chiun.

"Most assuredly."

The other source Chiun finally tracked down was a regional administrator who claimed to be the first one to call for Indians in those jobs.

And where, asked Chiun, did the administrator get the idea?

"It is mine. I thought of it. I am a man who is being watched in Delhi itself, most assuredly," said the administrator.

"And I am a friend of the prime minister. And he blames whoever thought of this as a walking disaster, an affront to the nation, an embarrassment to India because it makes people believe Indians can't run things."

"But it's the whites who are responsible. Everyone knows that. The lawyers know that. The people know that. The press knows that."

"As a friend of the prime minister, I blame you."

"Not me."

"Then who?"

"I will not say."

"A son?"

"I have no sons."

Remo started the upside-down treatment again, but Chiun raised a frail-looking hand.

"Please, don't be so uncivilized. Besides, a Master of Sinanju should not put his hands on anyone unworthy of the glorious death we deal."

"Nothing glorious about death. Death is death."

"You're so American," moaned Chiun.

The administrator left the room, asking them to wait, and Remo chafed at being thwarted in his desire to apply physical incentives. But shortly Remo saw that Chiun was right. For the administrator came back, saying he himself wanted to hear from the prime minister. If he were being accused of something, he wanted to defend himself.

"And who have you been speaking to?"

"No one. Only my wife," said the administrator. And that night Remo and Chiun visited the wife in the gardens of her house, among the fragrant blossoms and the fishponds.

At first she begged not to be beaten. Then, seeing she was not going to be harmed, she assumed the American and the Oriental were weak and threatened to call her husband. When this didn't work either, she cast a longing glance at the handsome American with the high cheekbones and mentioned her husband wouldn't be home for hours.

"Most beautiful and tempting maiden," said Chiun to the plump Indian wife, "as tempting as your beauty is, we must pursue a different course at this moment, to regret forever the losing of this rare moment of rapture in your splendid arms. Forgive us, we must be about your prime minister's business."

"The prime minister?"

"He is watching your husband closely for promotion."

"Then it was the right decision."

"Of course, beautiful maiden," said Chiun. "But we know there are evil forces about that would harm him. It was not the decision that was bad but the person behind it. And we know she is not bad either."

"You know so much, wise one. Yes, it was not me. It was a voice."

"And who was attached to the voice?"

"It is a strange thing. It came from strange places. It came from metal. But there was no one in the metal."

"I see. And what did it say?"

"It mentioned that my husband was being overlooked in Delhi because whites still held the important jobs in the International Carborundum & Phosphate factory."

"Ah, thank you," said Chiun, and when they left the house with the pastel exterior walls, Chiun said he had expected to find everything they had found that day. One only had to look at the mountains to know they would find all this. And he was disappointed to see Remo did not get that message when he was instructed to look at the mountains.

"I don't understand," said Remo.

"Obviously, when beggars are more important than your beloved teacher, the man who found you as nothing with white habits and made you into a Master of Sinanju, then you would of course not understand."

"Get off my back. What did I miss?"

"Something as obvious as the mountain. The gas was more deadly because it was kept in a bowl of mountains. The gas was released because the wrong people were put in charge. The wrong people were put in charge because an editor was struck in his ego and a wife was struck precisely and exactly in her ambition for her husband."

"I followed. What the hell does that have to do with the mountains?"

"The person we cannot find, the voice from nowhere, knows how things work."

"Well, that's obvious," said Remo.

"You missed it, as you missed the mountains," said Chiun.

Since the hotel was filled with American journalists and investigating engineers, Remo and Chiun accepted the hospitality of the plant manager, Rashad Palul, who lived in a house with twenty servants just as though he were a British official.

There were guest rooms and servants for Remo and Chiun. Flowers adorned the doorways. Cool water was placed at their disposal. A footman fanned their brows.

"And you," said Chiun, "still like America. . . ."

"All these servants make me nervous."

"Yes. You are only comfortable with machines doing your bidding. You like steel and microchips and engines. But when a warm human being attempts to serve you, you are revolted. I am up against invincible ignoranace," said Chiun.

And that night he went to sleep saying nothing more to Remo, hoping that if he kept him in India long enough the boy would learn something of a superior civilization.

In the morning there was a great commotion in the dining room. An American engineer was making a ruckus with Rashad Palul.

He had a Midwestern twang that could penetrate concrete. His name was Robert Dastrow. He had short, almost crew-cut blond hair, wire-rimmed glasses, and a white shirt with a tightly knotted blue tie. His sleeves were rolled up and his gray pants were smudged with engine grease. Four pencils, two pens, a slide rule, and a calculator bulged from his shirt pocket.

He was gathering information about the disaster and he seemed to know Cyclod B in detail, what went wrong, and what could be done to prevent further accidents. He wanted to know first, however, who Remo and Chiun were. He did not like strangers hanging around while he discussed company business.

"They are never strangers in my house," said Palul. "They are friends. Glorified and welcomed."

"Yeah, well, you can keep your glory business. I have to work with details. Where are they?"

"Sleeping," said Palul.

"No we're not," said Remo, entering the room.

"Good. Who are you?" said Dastrow.

"The voice of Christmas past. Who are you and what are you doing here?"

"I'm an engineer. Dastrow's the name. Robert Dastrow. D like in Diameter, A like Aerial, S like Sine, T like Trigonometry, R like Radius, O like Orbit, W like Wrench."

"Do you have to talk to communicate? Your voice is the most unpleasant thing I've ever heard."

"It's clear, isn't it?" said Dastrow. It sounded like a hundred wires being rubbed simultaneously. Remo's skin turned to gooseflesh at the sound.

"All right. What do you want? Just get out of here."

"Most people feel that way about me," said Dastrow cheerfully.

"Just ask and then go."

"You're investigating this for who?"

"A consulting firm," said Remo.

"That's another word for your not wanting to tell

me. All right, I can understand that. I've been looking around at the fine people of this fine country,"
said Dastrow. "A friendly, decent people you might
find anywhere in Wisconsin, Michigan, Minnesota,
or Indiana."

"Make it brief."

"You fellows seem to know your way around. You
get along with the natives. You were all over. Everyone who was anyone seemed to end up in Mr. Palul's
office with you. Everyone but a housewife you visited. Golly, you certainly are experienced travelers."

"What do you want?" said Remo, toying with the
idea of collapsing the man's larynx. If he collapsed
the larynx, the twang would not resonate on his
eardrums. He wondered if Chiun minded it as much
as he.

It was not the Midwest accent that bothered Remo.
He liked it. But this man seemed to be cutting glass
with every word he spoke.

"I just have one request, from a fellow engineer.
Would you fix this Roentgen gauge? It's microchip-
activated, of course."

"What?" said Remo, looking at a small metal box
with a window and a gauge on it. "I don't know what
that is."

"How about your fine friend?" asked Dastrow.

"He doesn't know mechanical things that well either. We're social-environment consultants."

"All righty. Thank you for your time," said Dastrow
with the same unflagging cheery boosterism with
which he seemed to greet everyone and everything.

As he left the house, he told Palul that a little
grease under the latch would probably save it for five
more years. And that he should look at rewiring the

house. The Indian climate was not kind to electrical equipment.

He also fixed an old Mercedes truck on his way out the driveway, a truck a driver was having trouble getting started, just by seemingly touching one wire to the other.

"Who was that?" asked Chiun.

"No one," said Remo.

"That is just who we are looking for," said Chiun.

6

Robert Dastrow whistled while he worked. He knew it bothered people but he always bothered people. Robert Dastrow bothered everyone but his parents.

Robert understood early that he was never going to win a popularity contest. At school dances he was the one who made sure Grand Island Nebraska High School had a public-address system that didn't make whooming noises. He did not have dates. Not that he didn't ask. Not that he didn't approach the problem in a systematic manner.

In fact, because he was so systematic he knew there wasn't a single girl who would go out with him, except perhaps the most beautiful one in school. Unfortunately, she was the one always involved in social causes. She was willing to go out with him as a favor.

"I didn't want favors from anyone, least of all someone I might want to marry and raise a family with."

"I just was willing to go out with you. I didn't mention anything about marriage."

"I don't want favors. I don't want favors from anyone. I don't need favors."

"Well, I do feel sorry for you."

"I don't want people feeling sorry for me. I am the most capable person you have ever met. And if you hitch up to me, I'll make you rich. You'll never want for anything."

"Actually, Robert, I'm sorry to say, the only thing I want from you is to spend absolutely no more than an evening with you."

"Keep your favors. You'll see. I'll be the most employable graduate of this high school."

"I'm sure you will, Robert. Everyone says you know how to make anything work."

"And someday I'll know how to make people work, too. You'll see. I'll have the most beautiful women."

Robert was only partly right. He ultimately did get beautiful women, but his career did not go smoothly at all. Despite his high marks in both high school and college, despite the fact that he successfully held many jobs to work his way through his degree, despite the fact that he scored at the very highest level on engineering aptitude, Robert Dastrow was virtually unemployable in the United States of the 1970's.

Every interview was almost the same. The personnel officer would be impressed with the young graduate and his high marks. He would be impressed with the young man's alertness, enthusiasm, and energy.

And then he would ask what Robert's specialty was.

"I just make things work," Dastrow would say. "I know how to make things work."

"Design engineering then?"

"Well, no. I'm not all that good at inventing. But you show me something somebody else has made and I'll show you how to make it work perfectly. I'll show you what's right or wrong about it. What's good and bad about it. I'll make it go. I'll make it hum. I'll make it buzz."

"I see. Do you have any marketing experience? That's big. Engineers who have marketing experience are always in demand for top jobs."

"Not my cup of tea," said Robert.

"If you know how to make things work, then you know what to sell about them. Sales. A sales engineer is the best paid of all engineers."

"Once had a newspaper route. Had to give it up. Couldn't afford to keep buying newspapers. Only people I ever sold a copy to were my parents. I couldn't sell an ice cube in the Sahara," said Dastrow.

"I see. Well, do you have a sense for structure then? We can use structural engineers."

"Not especially."

"How about environment? An environmental engineer?"

"Sorry. Just know how to make things work. I see your clock is broken," said Dastrow. He took a little screwdriver from his pocket and within moments had the desk clock humming again.

"You can't tell me you don't need a man like that," said Robert.

"Unfortunately, that's just what I'm telling you," said the personnel manager.

And so did many others. Because in the America of the 1970's the rage was not to make things work, but to make them more beautiful, more modern, and cheaper to produce.

The engineers who got the jobs were those who dealt in theory. As one company put it to young

Dastrow, "You should have seen the handwriting on the wall. At most engineering schools, they've closed the machine shops. Nobody cares whether something works well or not because they're designing new ones anyway. It's not important that it work. It's important that it's new. That it's cheap to make, and attractive."

Robert Dastrow, with his degree in engineering, spent the first year of his employable life as a messenger. And then an accident changed his life and ultimately helped change America too.

While visiting a relative in California he noticed a car go out of control. Robert saw the steering-wheel bearings were obviously misaligned. Anyone could see that. It was the manufacturer's fault.

Being from the Midwest, he shared this knowledge with anyone who would listen. Every other witness to the accident suddenly claimed not to see a thing.

A young lawyer, who just happened to hear an ambulance and just happened to be taking the identical route for the last fifteen blocks of the trip to the accident site, and just happened to stop to see what was going on, heard Robert Dastrow talking.

"Would you swear to it in a court of law?"

"Sure. It's the truth," said Dastrow. "But I've got to return home to Nebraska tomorrow. I may have a job. I'm not specifically saying I have a job. I'm not stating it is a sure thing. But golly, it looks good. Looks real good. Looks wicked good."

"I understand," said the lawyer. "I would be the last one to expect you to hang around Los Angeles for a trial when it's costing you money. I would be the last one to expect you to pay money out of your own pocket. But I think I could arrange a little per-diem payment for you, just to stay around."

"Is that legal?" asked Dastrow.

"If you get it in cash, and no one knows, and you don't tell anyone, and I don't tell anyone, there's nothing illegal about it."

"Sounds fishy to me," said Robert Dastrow. "Sounds like a bribe to me," said Dastrow.

"What's your name?"

"Dastrow. Robert Dastrow," said the unemployable engineer, and then sounding like a thousand steel guitars twanging their ugliest notes, he spelled out his name.

"Robert, I'm a lawyer. The law is not open-and-shut like laymen think. Nothing is illegal unless a court and the written law say it is illegal. That's the law. No court ever ruled on anything it didn't know."

"But concealing the truth doesn't make it less than the truth."

"Robert, we're talking about five thousand dollars in cash, minimum."

Robert Dastrow thought about truth and honesty. He thought about the values of his small Midwestern city. He thought about how he had been raised. Five thousand dollars would indeed go a long way toward a comfortable life in Grand Island.

"You said minimum."

"More if we win, Robert," said the young lawyer, who brought him back to his office to take a deposition. It was a storefront with some Spanish written on the front in case a passing Latino might need legal help.

There were two pieces of furniture, a chair and an old scarred wooden desk. On that wooden desk young

Nathan Palmer took down a deposition from Robert Dastrow.

His other two partners listened in amazement as he described the make and the car and how he could tell the ball bearings in the steering system were not properly aligned.

"Genius," said Arnold Schwartz, who recognized mathematical excellence.

"Interesting," said Genaro Rizzuto, "but will it hold up in court?"

As a test all three of them went at Robert Dastrow for two hours, trying to break him. But when it came to the workings of a mechanical object, Robert was not only at home, he was king. He even explained how some engineers might try to defend the structure of the automobile. And he refuted those defenses for the three lawyers.

At the end, Palmer, Rizzuto, and Schwartz were numb from talk of valves, ball bearings, balance, and structural design. Robert was fresh as a daisy and still talking.

What they learned from this young Midwest engineer who didn't have a job was that they would put the manufacturer on trial on behalf of the plaintiff.

The auto company took one look at Dastrow's deposition, passed it to their engineers, and the following morning not only agreed to the largest out-of-court settlement in the history of the industry, but promptly hired Palmer, Rizzuto & Schwartz on a large retainer. This meant that the firm and its technical support, namely its star witness, would never be able to act against them again.

The old desk went into a glass case, and Robert Dastrow received a personal retainer from the law firm of a hundred thousand dollars a year. If Robert had any residual moral qualms, they died after his first really good date. Of course the date had been arranged by a dating service in Los Angeles and the beautiful young woman seemed to smile at anything and everything, but she was a woman. She was beautiful. And Robert Dastrow was no longer poor or lonely.

The second thing he did after establishing human companionship of sorts was to build a machine shop in the basement of his new home back home in Grand Island. Unfortunately Grand Island did not have dating services, since in their lack of sophistication they called women providing companionship for money a form of prostitution.

But before he could get his machine shop running, he was visited by the three young lawyers. They were all desperate. Mr. Palmer had just come back from his honeymoon, which had ended in divorce. Mr. Rizzuto had spent a week in Las Vegas and now his income for the next three years was owed to people who collected either their money or pieces of the debtor's body. And Schwartz, violently adamant about the stupidity of the American investor and how idiots ruined the stock market, had just lost his home, everything in it, and his last extra pair of shoes.

"Golly, how'd you fellas spend so much money so quickly?" laughed Robert.

"That's not the point," said Schwartz. "The point is how we can make more."

"The point is how we can make you even richer," said Palmer. "How would you like to buy your own linear accelerator? How would you like your own atomic clock? How would you like anything in the world you fancy just to tinker with?"

"A bimetric deep-sea evaluator?" asked Robert.

All three young lawyers nodded, although none of them knew what it was. Palmer had read about the linear accelerator in a magazine on the flight to Grand Island from Los Angeles. He knew it had something to do with atoms. He knew it was expensive. He knew it might interest a nerd like Dastrow. He was, it turned out, very right about this.

"Well, there's no such thing as a bimetric evaluator," laughed Robert, slapping his knee.

"Whatever there is you want, you can get. What we need is for you to follow accidents with us and find the ones where a major rich company is at fault," said Palmer.

"Not the best use of your time, gentlemen. Best use of your time is knowing where the accidents will happen."

"You thought about this already?" asked Palmer.

"Just now. As I see it, fellas, once there's an accident there sure is a lot of competition for the cases, and everyone really starts sort of even, don't you think?"

"Maybe," said Rizzuto. He didn't like the idea of this hayseed telling him his business.

"Why start even?" asked Dastrow.

"Why not start even? Are you saying we didn't go to top-notch law schools or something? Is that what you're saying?" asked Schwartz. "Because if you're saying that anybody from a mail-order college is—"

"Not sayin' that at all, sir," said Dastrow. "But let's not waste time. You want lawsuits you're going to get, and lawsuits you're going to win. You don't have all the clients you need or you wouldn't be chasing ambulances."

"We're not ambulance chasers," said Schwartz.

"We most certainly are," said Palmer, thinking

about his divorce settlement. "Let's hear what you have to say."

"The way to work this best," said Dastrow, "is to begin with the inside track. Now, my happening by was an accident. The ball bearings being wrong was an accident. Accidents are not how things work well."

"What are you suggesting?" asked Palmer.

"These companies, big companies, don't really care how things work. They don't. I'd be a rich man if they did. I wouldn't have been working in a crummy messenger job. Now, if I told you I didn't hold this against them, I would be the biggest liar in the world. I hate them. I hate them with all my heart. With all my soul. I hate them deep in the marrow of my bones. I want them to pay for it."

"Just retribution," said Rizzuto.

"A cause to make the world safer for all mankind," said Schwartz, his voice ringing with emotion. That would be a good line for Rizzuto to sum up with somewhere.

"Go ahead," said Palmer.

"What say we predict the accidents because we know exactly how the things are not going to work?"

"How do we know that?" asked Palmer.

"Leave those little mechanical details to me. You don't want to know that. You just want to know how the accidents are going to happen and be prepared before they do. And this time don't take some silly retainer from an auto company so you can't sue them again."

"The man makes sense," said Schwartz.

"He's going to turn company negligence against them. The big bastards of the world are going to have to pay the little guy."

"How are you going to do it?" asked Palmer.

"That's not the question," said Dastrow. "The question is how are you going to pay me a million dollars in advance?"

"Impossible," said Schwartz. "Even I couldn't figure out how to leverage that much."

"You're sucking blood from the veins of your friends and allies," said Rizzuto.

"You'll get it," said Palmer.

The three lawyers left Grand Island muttering among themselves but with a new respect for Robert Dastrow. No one was calling him a hayseed anymore. In fact, when he came up with his first multiple accident and the money began to flow in, the word "genius" just naturally attended their descriptions of him.

Robert's first project was what would become known in legal circles as the venerable bumper-tank cases. To a layman it would seem impossible that a major auto company would design a car in which the rear bumper contained the most explosive element in the entire vehicle.

To Robert it was easy. He insinuated himself into the professional circles of the car designers and came up with better solutions to their problems. Robert Dastrow simply showed that if the rear bumper were to double as the gas tank, the car would have the distinctive expensive design of the "bubble back" and be three hundred dollars cheaper to make, and to boot, there would be more room inside the car. Cheaper, roomier, prettier, the little cars went out into the market and sold like firecrackers. That was also the way they blew up.

And Palmer, Rizzuto & Schwartz was there with ready proof of the fault of the design, even with some inside papers from an engineer who had been

fired when he warned that putting the gas tank in
the bumper was an invitation to disaster.

The hundreds of people who died or were badly
maimed in these accidents quickly learned of a law
firm that seemed to have the company dead to rights.

There was even a television investigative report on
the car and Rizzuto appeared for the partners.
Schwartz worked out the words to be said, and Palmer
worked out the fact that they had to use this television
program to advertise themselves nationally as the
one law firm that could win the big judgments against
the manufacturer.

When Robert Dastrow saw his first ugly picture of
a burn victim, he had his first regret. This poor girl
could never get her face repaired or her body mended.
Her parents were gone, and she was alone.

Dastrow thought about this for all of twenty minutes, and then realized that the art of making things
work was to know what could not be changed. He
couldn't bring back the dead, but he could certainly
buy himself a cyclotron. With this new arrangement
with the greedy lawyers in Los Angeles he would
now have the entire world to tinker with.

And all the American manufacturers who had no
use for Robert Dastrow, the young man who only
wanted to make things work, would now be shown
up for what they were. He would see their embarrassed faces on television as reporters interviewed
engineers and asked how they could design a car that
worked more like a bomb than transportation.

He would see aircraft designers get hauled over
the coals for a faulty wing structure. He would see
contractors sued out of business because they didn't
know how to lay concrete properly. He would be
vindicated and he would be rich.

And of course, everything worked the way Robert Dastrow had planned.

And since tinkering was life to him, when he noticed his main source of revenue under a new form of attack, he just had to find out what it was.

While International Carborundum & Phosphate and the international media looked at the valves in the Gupta plant, only two people looked at the real cause of the accident. They had spoken to the newswriter and ultimately the wife who goaded her husband into violating the basic rule of how to make anything work: If it ain't broke, don't fix it.

What he had done was to use the social structure to convince most of the people in the city that the administration was broken because it used Americans in previously undesirable jobs.

And the Oriental and the American who did not really have credible cover stories found that out within one day.

None of his work had ever been discovered so quickly. And of course as any good tinkerer knew, Robert Dastrow had to find out what was going on here. Who were these two new people doing the right things?

Did they have the same abilities that he did? A simple test proved they did not, when neither of them could fix the gauge. Therefore there had to be something else they had, and Robert Dastrow would have to figure it out, before he killed them. He had no doubt that he would. There wasn't anything in the world he couldn't figure out. He knew how everything worked.

The remnants of families in Gupta crowded around waiting for their meager emergency rations, wondering why all the foreigners were coming to them and telling them they were going to be rich.

They cared for their survivors and prayed that this thing would never happen again. In their own minds they believed that they were cursed and therefore some of them were embarrassed.

But a few older women found out that when they cried before the cameras they could at times get a bowl of rice. And so they cried more, and kept crying until their families were fed. Sometimes there were too many women crying in front of the cameras, and that drove down the reward. Little wars between the surviving Indian women developed as to who would have crying rights before which cameras.

Stories were other things. The people quickly found that those who had the most gruesome stories to tell were the ones who were visited most.

But all of this enterprise was nothing compared to the savior of Gupta and what he did for the people there. He brought rice, he brought doctors, he brought promises of rich compensation for the evil done to them by the American factory. He told them they should not let the Americans get away with it.

He was an American himself and he knew how bad the Americans could be. He was here to make them rich, to give them rice for the rest of their lives. Naturally, the offer sounded too good and no one signed up right away. But when he returned with the blessings of some high government officials, the survivors all happily lined up to give their palm prints as signatures to a contract that said he would give them ten percent of all he earned from making the American factory pay.

His name was Genaro Rizzuto, and he bet them all he would win.

Remo and Chiun found this out the second day they were there, but they had great difficulty talking to the people. Gupta was now an official international disaster, and being labeled as such attracted more stars than Remo had ever seen in one place.

Chiun pointed them out. He counted fourteen movie stars with their own camera crews, each posing with the same blinded woman, seven actors with current series on television, and a multitude of American organizations.

There were the directors of Aid to the Famished, International Help, Pity the Children, Save All Humanity, End Racism, Fight Racism, and International Alliance Against Racism. Starring in all this was a woman dressed like an untouchable who had just scavenged through a dime-store garbage can left outside the plastics department. Her eyes were shaded neon green. Her hair looked like a swamp that had gotten caught in a yellow-spray-paint machine, and her clothes were as tattered as though she had been the center of attention at a ragpickers' convention.

"There's Debbie Pattie," said one TV newsman who had already gotten his tear shots for the day. "She's new. She's not known for social causes."

Immediately a crowd formed around the young singer.

She was used to people forming crowds around her. What she was not used to was being ignored. And past the row of poor huts the victims lived in she saw two men, one Oriental and one white, who were not even bothering to look her way.

She made fifteen million dollars a year, was on the cover of almost every major magazine in the West, and she was of absolutely no interest to these two. This she spotted despite the fifteen microphones in her face, cameras whirring behind them.

"I soytinly don't need no more publicity in case yer asking," she said with a New York accent that advertised itself better than Broadway. "I'm here to help da people. All right? Whyn't youse guys go talk to da people. Dare the ones what's sufferin' around here."

"What do you think of the negligence of American factories?"

"I'm against anything that hurts," said Debbie. "What hurts people is what I'm against. I hate unhappiness and they oughta outlaw it."

"Do you think America has failed to outlaw unhappiness because it's racist?"

"I don't know. I know the people of Gupta need our help. And I'm here to see what I'm singin' for. We're gonna save the people. All us rock stars and singers are going to save the people of the world and we're gonna start here for the people of Gupta. Ain't no reason they should suffer and die just 'cause they was born here. They gotta get treated fair, see?"

"Since when has your new philosphical approach taken over your career?"

"I always believed this stuff. 'Cept youse guys never asked me about that."

Debbie left a half-dozen television reporters commenting on how she was showing new and deep spiritual feelings, how she was revealing a political sensibility she never had before. However, she wasn't considered too knowledgeable about international politics because she had failed to blame everything on America.

Debbie excused herself from her agent, her manager, the reporters, the guides, and the Indian constabulary to walk down the muddy street toward the two men who hadn't even glanced over at her.

The Oriental, in a gold kimono, was talking in the native language to two old men who were describing something with their hands. The younger white man, the attractive one with a sense of being able to do anything a woman might want, or perhaps anything he wanted for a woman, was listening. Debbie shook the multitude of bangles around her neck to make some noise. She also shook a large part of her amply endowed body. She did not believe in bras or panties.

Neither the Oriental nor the white looked up. The white man had found two Indian children to whom he gave money.

"I'm for charity too," said Debbie.

"Good," said the white man. "Why don't you buy yourself some decent clothes then?"

"Hey, you know who I am, wise guy?"

"Somebody who needs a good wash and possibly a simonize. Where did you get that color hair?"

"Does the Chinaman know who I am?"

"He's Korean, and I don't think so."

"If this wasn't so insulting I'd laugh. It's really funny, you know? Really funny. Do you know who you're ignoring, Mr. Nobody? I ain't never heard of you."

"What's bothering you?" said Remo.

"You, wise guy. You," said Debbie, poking him in the chest. The chest muscles seemed to catch at her purple fingernails. She noticed the Korean had even longer fingernails than she did. She wondered how he kept them that way.

"Well, then leave," said Remo.

"What'cha doin' here? Whose agent are ya?"

"If you knew, little girl, I'd have to kill you," said the white man with a friendly smile indicating that perhaps he was joking. But Debbie felt a tingling sense of danger.

"I'm here helpin' dese people. I don't just throw a coupla bucks at kids. I'm gonna earn 'em millions. Make 'em rich. Show da world how to treat people. You know much about music?"

"Not much," said Remo.

"That explains it," said Debbie. "No wonder. I'm a big rock star. Youse guys heard about rock, ain't cha?"

"Music?" said Remo.

"Yeah. Music. Maybe you heard my songs but don't know it's me, right?"

"Could we do this some other time?" said Remo.

"Hey, I'm the most desired woman in the world. Don't you brush me off, punk. You hear?" said Debbie. She pushed her fingernail into him again. For the last three years since her hit single "Rack Me, Rip Me" shot her to the top of the charts, she had discovered two ways to get anything she wanted, legal or illegal. One was to ask for it and the other was to demand it. Now she was demanding.

And there was a person actually refusing. He was saying no to Debbie Pattie.

"Hey, what's your name? You don't have to kill me if you tell me that."

"It's Remo. Leave me alone or stand downwind."

"Wise guy. What'cha make, Remo?"

"I make myself happy."

"Money, jerk."

"I don't count it," said Remo.

On hearing that the Korean sighed but continued

his conversation with the old men of the village. Even though she didn't understand the language, Debbie Pattie knew the old men were telling the Korean they didn't know the answers he sought. Their shoulders shrugged and their worn brown faces wrinkled in dismay. She thought they were cute, the way they squatted in the Indian dust. But the wise guy was absolutely beautiful. He seemed to move gracefully even when standing still.

"You wanna work for me? I'll pay you more than ya gettin' now."

"Hey, kid. Leave us alone. You don't even know what we do."

"I know I can buy you, punk."

"Well, you're wrong. So good-bye."

"You know how many guys'd kill demselves just to touch me once? So how come you don't even ask me about myself? Ask me what I sing. Ask me what I do. How about it?"

Debbie transferred the peach-sized wad of gum to the other side of her mouth. Remo noticed even the gum was off-color.

"Will you go then?"

"Yeah. I'll go."

"All right, what do you sing?"

And there in a side street of Gupta, India, Debbie sang the first few bars of her new smash hit, "Collapse." The Indians who didn't leave immediately covered their ears instead. Remo stood transfixed. He thought she was having a fit. Chiun glowered at her interruption.

"Okay. Thank you. Good-bye," said Remo.

"That song made me three million bucks," said Debbie.

"Did they bribe you to stop?" asked Remo.

"You know, you're impossible. You don't know who I am. You don't know who you're talkin' to. You don't know nothin'. That's ignorant. You're ignorant. You and your old friend there. Ignorant. Uneducated. So buzz off, I'm leavin'."

In a whirl of off-colored bangles and layers of rags, Debbie Pattie turned to leave.

"Genaro Rizzuto said there'd be people who hated you just for doin' good," she snorted.

Remo looked up from the little children. "Is he a lawyer?"

"A decent one, too. Not just a little money grubber like in show business. A decent human being, part of people helpin' people. Not like you."

Remo trotted after Debbie in the dusty street of Gupta.

"Look, I may have made a mistake. I don't know rock music. I don't know how those things work."

Debbie waved her hands in the air, signaling she wanted to be left alone.

"I want to apologize for being rude," said Remo.

"I don't want to know you because you're ignorant. An idiot. An uneducated idiot. That's what youse guys is."

"You're right. Rizzuto is part of a law firm, isn't he?"

"One of the best. Get lost."

"You don't mean that," said Remo. He was going to work on her sensory system but he wanted to do it from upwind. He didn't know what she bathed herself in, but whatever it was, it was putrid. Now that he was willing to be friendly she wanted no part of him. He glanced back and saw Chiun silently, like the wind, move up the street toward him and the rock star.

In Korean he told Chiun this girl knew one of their targets was around, but he couldn't get her to talk. He had insulted her in some way.

"In what way?" Chiun asked in Korean.

"I told her to get lost," said Remo.

"Sometimes people can take that in a negative way," said Chiun in Korean, and then in English he called out after Debbie Pattie in what Remo recognized as one of those awful ung poems praising all nature and the power of the universe. Unusually, though, he did so in English translation.

"O radiance, that renews for all eternity. O shower of glory that blesses the little people beneath her, whose divine countenance radiates eternity and all-consuming power, we bless your eternal breath."

Debbie Pattie stopped in her tracks. She turned abruptly to Remo and Chiun.

"Yeah. Now that's a friggin' hello, already. Did you hear that?" she said, pointing to Remo.

"I heard it."

"He's a friggin' gentleman. You're a jerk, but a cute jerk."

"What wisdom," said Chiun with a little bow.

Debbie Pattie posed in a grotesque parody of a statue, her head cocked to one side and one arm up, the wrist dangling limply. She looked Chiun and Remo up and down, and came to a decision.

"I like youse guys. You're hired. Go to my manager. He'll get you on the payroll. You, the young one, be in my van with your clothes off in a half hour. I may be there. I may not. Stay ready. Okay?"

"Excuse me, most gracious maiden," said Chiun, who was not about to endorse any union between his

Remo and some painted hussy who might be diseased or, worse, bear a child without Chiun knowing her lineage.

Remo, Chiun knew, was fond of that slothful and self-indulgent habit even found in the Orient, of copulating for pleasure. This to Chiun was as ridiculous as eating food not for its nourishment but for its taste. In either sense, however, this jangling ragpicker in front of them was totally unsuitable.

"Excuse me, most gracious maiden, but I have a calling of a different nature. However, if ever there should be a woman in our lives, of course it would be the most glorious, gracious, magnificent apparition we see before us now." Thus spoke Chiun to the famous rock star in the muddy streets of the Indian city of Gupta.

"I'll pay more," said Debbie. "I'm reasonable."

"I'm not for sale," said Remo.

"Why not? You know who you're turning down?"

"I didn't say I was turning you down. I said I'm not for sale."

And holding his breath, Remo moved in close to Debbie Pattie.

"You're all right. What's your name?" she asked.

"Remo."

"What kind of a name's dat?"

"White," said Chiun.

"And yours?"

"I am Chiun, Master of Sinanju."

"I like dat. You run Sinanju, huh?"

"No, I merely serve it, as I serve the world, as Sinanju has served the world throughout the ages."

"Ya see, dat's what I like. Doin' good. I'm into doin' good. Heavy. You know? Heavy into doin' good.

You think I ought to give these people a few bars of
my latest hit?"

"No. They're in enough trouble already," said
Remo.

Debbie shot him a dirty look, but Remo quickly
turned the subject to her friend Genaro Rizzuto, a
decent man who had come to Gupta like all the other
stars to help.

"We want to help too," said Remo. "I'd like to
meet him."

7

Nathan Palmer spotted the full extent of the disaster first. Rizzuto was on the scene in Gupta. Rizzuto could talk sparrows out of trees and he had brilliantly won over the government with well-placed lavish gifts, lined up the victims, and had one of the greatest negligence cases of all time aimed at one of the richest chemical companies of all time. Everything seemed perfect.

And then the little horrible fact of the paltry value of life in the third world reared its horrifying head, and Palmer was so panicked he canceled a date for the evening and called in Schwartz, who had to pry himself away from his stockbroker.

It was they, not their mechanical genius Dastrow, who had made the horrible mistake. He had done everything right, as always.

Schwartz was so furious when he entered their plush Century Park City offices that he almost broke the glass case protecting the Desk.

"Disaster in Gupta," said Palmer.

"I should hope so. That's what we make money on. We're going to make a fortune."

"That's what we're going to go to the cleaners on," said Palmer.

"You called me away from the one stock-market transaction that can make up for a lifetime of losses to make me listen to your pessimism?"

"Arnold, I probably saved you from bankrupting yourself for the rest of your natural life. What do you think happened in Gupta?"

"We started one of the greatest negligence cases of all time. We signed up an entire city as clients. We've got two thousand, two hundred and twenty deaths of heads of families, at least seven thousand children deprived of their lives, twenty-four hundred mothers whose love and support will be denied entire families, to say nothing of a slew of healthy young able-bodied young men and beautiful young women who will never bear children or enjoy the loves and lives of families," said Schwartz. "And I'm not counting the incalculable grief. Rizzuto is going to have those juries attaching every single asset of International Carborundum & Phosphate. It'll be come-and-get-it day."

Nathan Palmer shook his head sadly.

"There are two kinds of people in the third world. There are the handful who run things. They're very rich. Each of their lives is worth a fortune. But they don't need lawyers because they are the courts. They are the army. They are the government. And they already take a rakeoff from any industry that has a hope of surviving. These people are the money. Then there are the citizens of their countries, the ones these people attend the pricey conferences about."

"Yes," said Schwartz, adjusting his cuff because it had accidentally covered his gold Rolex.

"What do you think the value of a human life is in those countries?"

"You just can't put a price on a human life," said Schwartz angrily. "You've got to establish his earning power. What he means to a family. A corporation. Lots of things go into determining the value of a human life."

"In dollars and cents, Arnold," said Palmer. "What do you think we're talking about per head?"

"That's difficult to figure out. I would estimate . . ."

"Don't even bother. If we could get seven dollars a head out of the thousands who were killed in Gupta, we'd be lucky. Do you know what their government thinks?"

Schwartz was afraid to ask.

"Their government thinks that they *want* the factory there. The tragedy is of course a tragedy, but there are lots more people in India than there are chemical factories."

"What about Rizzuto whipping up popular resentment? He could make a bishop want to burn down a church. He's wonderful."

"And you're brilliant, Arnold. But the fact remains that angry mobs are all over the third world. They're commonplace. Don't mean a damned thing except to American television. If American televison weren't there, the governments would shoot down the people like so many mad dogs. Why do you think you don't have protests in Syria and Bulgaria? Show me a demonstration in Cuba that isn't in support of the government."

"What are you saying, Nathan?" asked Schwartz. He thought of that horror of horrors for one terrible moment: life without visible wealth, life with people finding out who you really were because there was nothing to throw in their faces before they could ask questions.

"I'm saying we are in hock up to our eyeballs for the money we paid Dastrow. I'm saying I don't know where we're going to go, or what we're going to do to make it."

It was at that moment that Arnold Schwartz in all his expensive clothes and jewelry showed Nathan Palmer why he was such a good partner. They were both overlooking one salient fact. Robert Dastrow to the best of their knowledge had never worked for anyone else. Why? He had only worked for them. Why?

"Because we paid him a friggin' fortune," said Palmer.

"He could have gotten that sort of money elsewhere. But he stayed with us. I say we reach out for him again."

"We have no money for him. He loves money."

"Ah," said Schwartz. "But why does he love it? It's never over till it's over."

"It's over," said Palmer.

"No it's not," said Schwartz, and he dialed the access number to Robert Dastrow. Sometimes Dastrow would answer immediately, and sometimes he would take hours or days. They never knew. But Palmer pointed out that every hour they waited cost them thousands in interest on the loans they had taken out to pay their genius.

Robert Dastrow phoned before evening, and Palmer and Schwartz didn't even know from which continent the call came.

"Robert," said Schwartz. "We've worked together a long time. We've been always forthcoming with your fees. We have a great deal of respect—"

"I don't for free," said Dastrow.

Palmer dropped his head in his hands. Schwartz

pressed on. They didn't have much more to lose. They could take out an even larger loan and let him invest it, but he knew that Palmer and Rizzuto lacked his mathematical genius and didn't trust the immutable laws which ultimately would prevail over the insanity of the U.S. stock market. So an even bigger loan was out of the question.

"Robert, we're broke. The Gupta thing didn't work out financially."

"I didn't think it would," said Dastrow.

"Then why did you do it?"

"Because it was absolutely safe, for one. You have to admit that. And for two, I wasn't sure. I was never much of a cost engineer. I gave you exactly what you asked for."

"We're in trouble now."

"Not really. I've been thinking about this for a couple of days. You're going to get back your money and maybe turn a handsome profit."

"You're a genius. How?"

"Your problem is that the life of the average citizen of the third world is worth roughly, as close as I can get it, between five and ten dollars, except in some African countries and Cambodia, where it's worth absolutely nothing. So where's your return? Not there, of course. What you have to do is move the case to America, where a life is worth something."

"Yes, but how?"

"It's already begun. You see, what's working here is an awful lot of public concern in just the place you need it. America. Therefore, get the trial moved to America."

"But it happened in India. No court in its right mind, so to speak, is going to accept a claim in America."

"Ah, you ought to be a tinkerer like me. You've hit on just the problem, and the solution is already under way. I have eliminated the need for any rationality. You see, you lawyer fellows don't really think things through. You think because something is irrational, you can't pull it off."

"What are you talking about?"

"I have eliminated the need for any common sense whatsoever."

"How on earth did you do that?"

"I used what was already there. You gentlemen are going to be the beneficiary of a public cause. It needs absolutely no reason whatsoever. Just emotion, and Gupta offers that. I have already told your man Rizzuto to get in on the big charity movement, something he can do well because he appeals to people's emotions. And it worked. Just listen to your own news: there's going to be a massive benefit for Gupta, and you're going to profit from it."

"Do you expect us to steal from a benefit? That's low."

"That and other things. Your man's job, as I outlined it to him, is to use the concert as a platform to get the case transferred to an American court, where you can clean up on human lives."

"Wonderful," said Schwartz. "I don't know how to thank you. I guess you have good reasons to keep us solvent."

"Not in the least," said Dastrow.

"But why have you only worked for us?"

"That is the secret of making things work. What works, works."

"And so you would see a danger in working for someone else, because there would be something new involved. Right? I thought so," said Schwartz.

"Not quite right. I don't have to work for anyone anymore. I have everything I need."

"Then why are you doing all this?"

"Because I want to find out how something works."

"I can't imagine anything you don't understand."

"Neither can I," came the twangy voice with the sunshine bounce. "That's why I'm so delighted to discover this mystery. And by the way, I'm going to save you to boot. It's good to have a challenge again."

"The new force you were talking about?"

"Yes."

"Are you going to do away with it?"

"Of course. That's why we're having the big benefit in America. That's why I told Rizzuto to be there, to use it. I'm not doing this for you, Mr. Schwartz. I never have. I need that benefit concert as much as you do."

It was called Save Humanity. Fifty rock stars joined together on one album and in one concert, which was to take place simultaneously in five cities around the globe. They were going to save humanity by saving the people of Gupta, who had been ravaged by modern technology.

The theme song was "Save," and the singers simply intoned the word over and over again. It went to number one on the pop charts the day it was released. Rock songs usually were inane, but this one was totally meaningless.

Many columnists were calling the Save Humanity effort the most meaningful movement in history.

For once, Remo and Chiun agreed.

"What does it mean?" they both asked.

Debbie Pattie had introduced them to her hangers-on as friends. When Debbie moved, she moved in caravans. She dressed like a beggar and moved like a king. She had five bodyguards, each of whom had attempted to keep Remo and Chiun at a distance. Now she had five hospital bills. No one had seen exactly how her bodyguards had received so many broken bones, but her accountant, who said he saw the whole thing, could have sworn that one of them tried to guide the old Oriental away from a doorway and the next thing anyone knew, he was on the floor screaming and they were calling for ambulances.

Remo and Chiun had taken over Debbie's guard duties. Remo had also offered to do the same for a good-looking lawyer named Genaro Rizzuto. He had been very friendly with Rizzuto, offering to help secure him a telephone whenever he wanted to phone his home office, wanting to know everything about him. He had made sure Rizzuto had gotten a room on the same floor that Debbie had rented in the Ritz Hotel of Chicago where the main concert was to be held.

Debbie had complained about this, since she liked to have a floor to herself, but she said she always had trouble denying anything to Remo. She usually said this while slumped in a chair with her legs spread. Remo would have thought this was a sexual offer except she always slumped in a chair with her legs spread, even as she was doing now, explaining the popularity of the song "Save."

"What does it mean?" she repeated. "It means everything. It means who we are and what we are."

"I don't understand," said Remo. The door to her suite was open, and he could see Rizzuto's door. Rizzuto had gone in there supposedly for an afternoon nap, along with four men and three decks of cards. The big benefit concert was to be that evening, and he was supposed to appear in it for some reason. How he had insinuated himself into a bunch of rock stars, Remo did not know. But it was worth finding out. He did not have anything on the trio of shysters in California, but this had to be the closest thing to a slipup they were going to make.

"We have to save ourselves, or who else will do it?" asked Debbie. "Right?"

"How?"

"By raising more money in one night than was ever raised before. Raising it for goodness instead of evil. Do you know that one fighter plane costs twenty million dollars? If that money were used for good instead of evil, think how nice the world would be." When Debbie Pattie was at her most earnest, a large part of her Brooklyn accent disappeared. The transformation was remarkable.

"I think Remo is asking how this money will do good," said Chiun.

"It's going to the people who need it instead of the people who already have it," said Debbie. She was repeating what she had heard. And she was annoyed that someone would dare bother her with such stupid questions. After all, if reporters never asked them what was going to happen to the money, why should friends like Remo and Chiun?

"Are they going to hand them dollar bills or what?"

"No, dammit. It's for a charity, you know. Like charity. Who knows what happens when you give for any charity? It does good, right? Better than paying taxes," said Debbie. She was sure that would get a positive response. All the reporters always laughed when she said that, and many said it showed she had a deep understanding of politics which she hid behind her simple songs.

"No," said Remo.

"Whadya mean, 'no'? No one says no. You don't say no, just no, like that," said Debbie. She was snarling.

"I'm saying no. Taxes are good. They pay to defend your country, keep your roads up, feed your people, support your allies. They're good. Who's getting the money from Save Humanity?"

"Humanity, asshole," yelled Debbie. "Tell him who humanity is. It's all of us. It's every one of us regardless of race, creed, or national origin. It's the babies and the mothers. It's the fathers and the brothers, it's you, man, and it's me, man."

"Anytime you want to really answer my question, feel free," said Remo.

"Tell him. You tell him," Debbie said to Chiun.

Chiun was busy pondering the selection of robes he might wear. Though he was not allowed onstage, Debbie had assured him he could stand in the wings.

"Listen to her, she makes sense," said Chiun, imagining how the pure black kimono would look with a single silver lotus blossom. He wondered if it would clash with the costumes of the rock stars. And then he gave up, realizing that everything clashed with what rock stars wore.

In Korean, Remo told Chiun he was not going to humor her like Chiun preferred to do.

And in Korean Chiun answered: "He who reasons with fools dresses in warm aspic."

"I stand for things, little father."

"The wrong things, Remo. Be nice to the girl. Then we can get on with this idiotic degradation of assassins' calling, this occupation termed detective work."

Remo glanced back at Rizzuto's door. He could

hear laughter in the room. He could also hear Rizzuto curse. The big concert was only a few hours away. He had to find out what Rizzuto's plans were for the concert before then. Why, he was not sure. But he was fairly certain that if he knew what Rizzuto was going to pull, he could be there to make sure some evidence for a court case could be unearthed.

Remo found the door to Rizzuto's room locked. With a careful pressure of the handle against the lock, he cracked the lock. Unfortunately he cracked it too hard. It shattered with the force of a grenade. The door flew open and three men ducked behind couches grabbing for shoulder holsters. The only one who didn't have a pistol was Rizzuto. He was playing cards for big stakes with three strangers who carried guns.

The piles of bills were naturally not in front of him, and his checkbook was open with a leaking fountain pen beside it. Remo thought it looked like it was bleeding.

Remo shut what was left of the door behind him.

"Hi, it was open, so I thought I'd just pop in."

"Who're you?"

"Friend of Rizzuto's."

"We're leavin'," said one of the men. "He can't bring in some backup."

"Get out of here, Remo. I gotta recover. They can't leave."

"Don't worry, they're not leaving," said Remo.

"We're leavin'," said the one who did not put his gun away.

"Well then, if you must, but don't take any money with you."

"We're leavin' with our dough, sweetheart," said the man with the gun.

"Because you have a gun?"

"Because we won it and yeah, because we got guns."

"Genaro, do you always play with strangers who have guns?"

"I didn't know they had guns until you crashed in," said Rizzuto.

Remo caught the thug's attention with a smile, which was enough distraction for him to slap the gun free. He also got the other guns as they reappeared from their holsters and put them in the middle of the table. Then he said they could all leave with their guns and money but he wanted to play a few hands of poker.

The three men looked at each other, stunned. They hadn't seen the hand that had disarmed them. They had moved for their guns, held out their guns, and then found them missing.

One of them couldn't believe it. He lunged for his gun in the middle of the table. Something sharp like barbed wire brushed the back of his palm, causing incredible pain. And yet there was no bleeding. There was just the stranger who had burst through the door, who had taken the guns so quickly they didn't see his hand move. And he was smiling. The gambler cradled the throbbing hand that the stranger had barely touched.

"I think we're going to play some cards," said Remo.

"I didn't know you gambled," said Rizzuto. If he had known that, he wouldn't have ignored the man all this time since Gupta, the man with too many questions Genaro Rizzuto did not want to answer.

"All the time," said Remo.

"What do you like to play? Stud? Five-card draw? What?"

"Poker," said Remo.

"They're all poker," said Rizzuto.

"The one with full houses and flushes," said Remo.

"They all have that. How much poker have you played?"

"Enough," said Remo. Actually he hadn't played cards for years. When he was a policeman, before he went through the phony execution to make him the man who didn't exist, before his training and new life with Chiun, he had played, for pennies and nickels, poker that had so many different wild cards and payoffs that the big hands wouldn't end in winners and losers but in heated arguments over the rules.

These men played a hard tight game for big money. They would never play a game with so many cards wild that there could be three straight flushes in one hand, the highest grouping of cards. And the only gambling game Chiun had taught him wasn't really a gambling game, but a Korean mental exercise originated by the Masters of Sinanju called Ka, or game of stones, from which the far cruder Japanese game of Go emerged.

"Sure I can play poker. Let's play the kind where you get five cards and nothing is wild."

"Five-card draw," said Rizzuto. The gamblers returned to the tables, exchanging quick glances. What the glances said was that they were soon going to win back their guns and anything else that was on the table from this lunatic who broke doors and moved so quickly no one saw him.

Before they began Remo had one question.

"Among the four suits, the highest suit is spades, right?"

They all nodded.

"You sure you know poker?" asked Rizzuto.

"Sure," said Remo. "Just one more question. Spades is black, right? But so is clubs. Clubs is the one with the bumps, not smooth rounded like spades. Spades are more heart-shaped. Right?"

"Right," said everyone.

"No limit with a C-note ante," said one of the gamblers.

"That's a hundred dollars," said Remo.

"Right," said everyone.

One of the reasons Remo lost his liking of money was that upstairs supplied all his needs, and there was no reason for him to accumulate anything. He moved around so much it was silly to buy a home. He never cared about cars, so the walking-around cash upstairs gave him tended to stay in his pocket for a long time.

He had twenty hundred-dollar bills almost as fresh as the day they were issued to him years ago. He put one into the middle of the table. Everyone else tossed in money, except Rizzuto, who put down an IOU, asking Remo if it were all right.

"These guys are my friends. They take my IOU's," said Rizzuto. As soon as one of the men began to deal, Remo could tell why they were so generous.

Someone else might simply have seen cards being shuffled, but Remo clearly saw each individual card, and he saw the aces move up the deck like a ladder with exactly three rungs—the other cards—between each ace.

Remo smiled and folded on the first hand. Rizzuto bet heavily. He had kings. He lost.

When it came time for Remo's turn to deal, the

hard part was reminding himself what were second-, third-, and fourth-highest hands.

He spread the cards out faceup in one sweep of his hand to see where each was, and then quickly collected the deck. With one hand moving several cards so rapidly it looked like shuffling, he moved the other hand, careful not to use so much speed that he burned the cards from friction; feeling the weight of each, the balance of each, the very power of the stability of the room, he got the cards in order, careful to give each man the right hand.

There was the formality of the cut, whereby one of the players, to avoid cheating and assure honesty, took half the deck from the top and put it on the bottom. As Remo picked up the deck to deal, he simply reversed the weighting of the cards, so that the deck went back to the way he arranged it. All three of the gamblers watched him closely. None of them saw him work the deck.

Strangely, none of them bet heavily. Only Rizzuto, who had the winning hand.

Rizzuto cursed his luck that the first time he got spades straight flush, no one else had anything to bet into him. And then Remo gave them all a little demonstration. He made them turn up their cards, something players never had to do, but encouraged to be honest by the promise of getting their wrists snapped if they didn't go along, they all complied.

When Rizzuto saw that one had a straight flush in clubs, one in hearts, and the third in diamonds, he realized something was wrong.

"They were waiting until they dealt so that they could be sure of winning. Genaro," said Remo, "these guys have been robbing you. They're con men. They're thieves. You haven't been gambling. You've been taken."

"They were the only action around," said Genaro.

"What action? It's losing," said Remo.

The three gamblers began easing their way away from the table, trying to get in position to make a lunge for the door.

"You forgot something," said Remo. "His money."

Quickly the gamblers pulled out wads of bills and laid them on the table along with a blizzard of white IOU's. Rizzuto collected them all.

"One more thing," said Remo. "Your money. The money he didn't have a chance to win. C'mon. It's a friendly game."

"Friendly, how? That's robbing," said one gambler.

"It's friendly because I'm not pulling your spinal cord out through your mouth," said Remo. "That's friendly, don't you think, Genaro?"

"I'd say so," said Rizzuto.

With a good two hours until showtime, Genaro suggested that since they were alone and still had a deck of cards, they play a little stud.

"You just saw how I fixed the damned deck," said Remo. "Do you really think you have a chance to win?"

"You wouldn't cheat me."

"Of course I would. Look, buddy. I may be the only friend you have across a table."

"Why are you doing this? Friends don't come across gambling tables."

"Because I see someone who wants to help. You're not just another shyster ambulance chaser. You're someone who cares. You wouldn't be joining this Save Humanity spectacular if you weren't."

"Two hands," said Genaro.

"I want to talk about saving people."

"I'll deal and then we know it will be fair. I never cheat."

"How did you hear about the Gupta disaster so quickly? And how did you know what was wrong so quickly?"

"Blackjack. One hand of blackjack. You can deal. The odds are with you. What's a hand of blackjack?" asked Rizzuto. His dark eyes were begging. "Ten seconds. Then I'll tell you. Anything you want to know. My love life. The inner workings of Palmer, Rizzuto & Schwartz. You name it. One simple hand. Do you know how to play blackjack? You deal one card down to me, one card down to you. Then I bet. I call for another card. Two simple cards. I keep calling for cards to get as close to twenty-one as possible. If I go over, that's it. I lose. What's the most cards you can possibly deal, seven, right? Seven cards, and then I tell you anything you want to know."

Rizzuto shot out the words like a machine gun and was shoving the cards into Remo's hands.

Remo dealt out a hand of blackjack, not expecting all that was promised. Rizzuto lost.

"Okay, I just want to know what you attribute your success at your firm to. You're probably the most successful negligence lawyers in the country. The reason I ask is I have an aunt who's really . . ."

"What're you doing with the cards?" asked Genaro, as horrified as if Remo had just thrown a baby out of a window.

"We played a hand. Now we talk," said Remo.

"What hand?" said Genaro with such vehemence that his gold jewelry tinkled on his dark hairy chest. "You don't play a hand of blackjack. You play a deck. How can I have a chance to win if I don't see what cards come up?"

"You said a hand. You didn't say a deck."

"I didn't say a deck," said Rizzuto, imitating Remo. "What's the big problem? Deal. We'll talk as you deal."

"You seem to have the best technical assistance in the business," said Remo as he dealt another hand. "I mean you really know what causes accidents. How do you know so quickly and so well? Is it you? Is it Schwartz? Is it Palmer?"

"Hit me," said Rizzuto, signaling for another card.

Remo would have loved to. He could have gotten everything he needed in thirty seconds by simply taking one ankle of one negligence lawyer and hanging the party of the first part out of the hotel window by the ankle of said party of the first part, until in maximum fear, party of the first part would divulge to Remo, the party of the second part, exactly how his law firm was raping America, immobilizing industries, and generally turning the protection of the law into an unbearable burden for the people.

But Smith had said no. Precisely because they were lawyers they had to be destroyed by legal means. It was the law that CURE was trying to protect. Remo thought momentarily of burying them all under lawbooks. He held up the card.

"We're good. That's all. You want us to take your aunt's case? You got it. Hit me."

Remo gave him his card. Rizzuto wanted another.

"Who deals with your technical people?"

"Palmer. Hit me."

Remo gave him another card. Rizzuto went over twenty-one and sat drumming his hands on the table. Remo dealt a card again. Rizzuto bet again. Remo held up the next card.

"What does Schwartz do?"

"Tactics. Palmer does strategy on the general idea

of what we should do. Schwartz shows how to do it. And on the big cases, I do it myself in a courtroom. I'm a trial lawyer. I'm wonderful. Another card, please."

Remo dealt. Then he dealt to himself. He won again by getting closer to twenty-one.

"Why would you say you are so successful? More successful than any single lawyer or law firm?"

"Because we know what we're doing and we'll take care of your aunt. We have law offices all over the country. We travel all over the world. When you get Palmer, Rizzuto & Schwartz, you get a world of protection. Now deal, dammit."

Remo played blackjack with Rizzuto for almost two hours, getting little information he felt he could use, but winning seventy-five thousand dollars without thinking about it. Ten thousand in cash and sixty-five thousand in IOU's.

He walked with Rizzuto to the giant auditorium, wired now to reach out live to the world. When they got to the aisle with screaming fans and televison cameras and paparazzi, Remo ducked into the crowd and moved through it, hidden by the dense sea of people. He caught up with Rizzuto by coming up on the blind side of a guard who was posted to ensure that no one crossed the line to be with the celebrities.

"Gambling's pretty expensive for you," said Remo.

"No. Not expensive."

"You lost seventy-five thousand dollars in two hours."

"You figure wrong. That was the total loss. But do you know how much was wagered in winning and losing, and going back and forth? Maybe almost a million dollars. I got a million dollars of action for seventy-five thousand. Now where else can you get a

return on your money like that? Take buying shoes
for my kid. Fifty bucks for a pair of shoes. That's it.
They're labeled fifty dollars. You pay fifty dollars,
good-bye. Now when you gamble, that money can
come back. For fifty dollars that I waste on a pair of
my kid's shoes I get maybe five hundred dollars in
action. And that's if I lose."

"You're a compulsive gambler, Genaro," said Remo.
This might be a weakness he could work on to get
some sort of legal case for CURE to transfer to some
prosecutor.

"No. I'm not a compulsive gambler."

"If you're not, who is?"

"People who are worse than me. There are guys
who will bet the clothes off their backs. I mean it.
Guys who get killed by loan sharks because they
borrow to pay loans from other killers."

"Where do you draw the line, then?"

"Right beneath me," said Rizzuto, who bet Remo
there was an odd number of performers on the stage.

Remo refused to bet. The stars were packed on
the stage like so many cattle. The lights in the center
of the auditorium were blinding, and the heat was
oppressive. But the stars all managed to look as
though they couldn't be happier, even when having
to quaff emergency water rations. It was like a mara-
thon run for the singers, except the singers had to
smile. Rizzuto wore a lavender tuxedo with a neon-
blue cummerbund and a diamond-studded bow tie.
On this stage he looked subdued. Remo tried to stay
near him, but he saw Chiun in the rear signaling to
him.

Debbie Pattie, who was going to do the last solo,
needed special wiring held by her bodyguards. Since
none of them were here after Remo got into a shov-

ing match with them, and since the new ones for some reason hadn't arrived yet, would Remo do the decent thing and carry Debbie's wires?

"Which ones?" asked Remo, looking at the dark tangle of wires.

"I don't know. My regular equipment didn't get here for some reason, and all this stuff is new. All I know is I have to have powerful amps on my voice and guitar or I sound like a squeaky little kid."

"Like at Gupta."

"Yeah. Although it's still real Debbie Pattie."

"I don't like gadgets."

"You know how many people would give an arm to be this close to me, Remo? Chiun, you tell him. You know what's going on."

"This is all craziness, Remo," said Chiun in Korean. "Why now do you balk at this added craziness? Carry the wires or we will have to keep talking to this little fool."

"Okay," said Remo in English.

"Thanks, Chiun. You're the decent one. You understand what I mean by saving the world."

"Until you know where the money goes you don't know what you're doing," said Remo.

"Why are you so negative? Even the reporters don't ask questions like that. Reporters never ask questions like that. They ask when I became so knowledgeable about world affairs, when I became so philosophical."

"You don't know until you know where the money goes," said Remo, and took a handful of Debbie Pattie's wires. They were thick, almost as wide as hot dogs, and they seemed to stick to his skin as he held them, as though they were covered with some form of gelatin. Remo looked around the stage to see if there were others like them, but there weren't. The others were the normal thin wires that didn't glisten with this strange substance on them. The closest thing to it in Remo's mind was the substance people used to make electrocardiograph electrodes more effective in reading the heart.

The first song was the now famous "Save." A hundred stars, amplified by a million megawatts, blared out that one word over and over again. "SAVE. SAVE. SAVE. WE SAVE. SAVE SAVE SAVE. PEOPLE SAVE. SAVE SAVE SAVE. WE SAVE. SAVE SAVE SAVE."

The crowd screamed. The singers screamed. The stagehands screamed. The noise onstage could have deafened people sitting outside the auditorium.

Chiun shouted into Remo's ear.

"White music."

"Not all white music is like this," Remo yelled back.

"Doesn't have to be. This is enough."

The noise went on for fifteen minutes. When it subsided to the level of an avalanche, an announcer called it the most meaningful experience of the twentieth century.

Then one of the singers introduced Genaro Rizzuto and Remo discovered what Palmer, Rizzuto & Schwartz had up its sleeve.

"We have here someone who is fighting for the poor," said the lead singer. "We have here someone who takes his care and concern into the field. This man was on the scene even before the doctors. This man was Gupta. This man was the suffering. This man was the dying. This man was the first to say 'save.' He said we couldn't let our brothers die anywhere in the world, or we would let them die everywhere."

The last piece of absurdity was met with hysteria, and when it died down the singer said, "I give you Genaro Rizzuto of the law firm of Palmer, Rizzuto & Schwartz. They care. They save. And they have an important message for you."

Rizzuto came forward among the bangles, the rags, the glitter, the heat, and the noise. And he too managed a big smile.

He thought of the thousands of yelling people as a jury, and in so doing he felt at home.

"I'm just a lawyer," yelled Rizzuto.

The crowd screamed back. One girl fainted and another desperately lunged forward to touch his shoes before she died.

It was then that Rizzuto realized the rock crowd was better than a jury.

"I am just a lawyer, and I just defend the rights of people to live safely, to live in peace, to live in an environment that doesn't kill them, to drive cars that don't maim them, to visit doctors who will not murder them with their incompetence. I am just a lawyer."

The crowd screamed its answer. "Save. Save. Save."

"And we went to Gupta so that these people, these poor people, would not suffer in vain. And what did we find? We found that the world does not care. The world does not care about a person if he's brown, if he lacks power, if he doesn't live in some white country. The world does not care."

"Destroy the world," screamed out one young man with a peace symbol on his T-shirt.

"No. Let us save the world," yelled Rizzuto, ripping off his tie and popping buttons off his shirt, then flinging his arms wide, his chest exposed like the other stars, the lights playing off his glittering teeth. "Save the world. Save. Save. Save."

"Save. Save. Save," the crowd yelled back.

"We cannot put a price on a life because of the color of a man's skin."

"No," yelled back the crowd.

"We cannot put a price on a person's life because of where that person was born."

"No," yelled back the crowd.

"Everyone has the same right to life that we have."

"Yes," yelled back the crowd.

"Everyone has a right to a life as good as everyone else's."

"Everyone."

"Here."

"Here," yelled back the crowd.

"In America."

"America," yelled back the crowd.

Now Genaro's voice hushed, forcing the people to strain to listen. "But I am sorry to say, my friends, that big rich corporations know how the world works. The little people, you and me, the people who suffer, don't know how the world works. The big rich corporations with their rich lawyers know that if they put a dangerous plant in a poor country, the lives of the poor won't matter that much. They know all lives are not equal. They know they can make money from the suffering of the poor. And they know they're going to get away with it."

"No," screamed the crowd. Someone called out for the death of all corporations.

"No," said Genaro. "We don't want them to die. We don't want them to collapse. We just want them to stop killing our planet, killing our brothers, and there's a way to do it."

"Do it," screamed the rock stars along with the crowd.

"We can say to them, 'Hey! Our brothers' lives are worth something. You can't keep killing our brothers and getting away with it.' We can say to them, 'You've got to pay for your misdeeds, just as if you did them in our home. Just as if you did them in San Francisco or New York City or here in Chicago. Our brothers are our brothers wherever they are.' "

And thus with the mob screaming "Save our brothers," Genaro Rizzuto brilliantly made a public appeal for change of venue. He started a mass movement to make crimes committed in a foreign land punishable in the home country of the corporation, because in America a life was not worth an average of seven dollars, but more like a quarter of a million, and the fifty percent Palmer, Rizzuto & Schwartz would collect on a quarter of a million dollars would be enough to pay for Palmer's love life, Schwartz's investments, and Rizzuto's willingness to gamble with strangers who carried guns and didn't bet on hands they didn't deal themselves.

Remo listened to all this and both he and Chiun sensed something else was at work here, something far more dangerous than a change of venue, something that was going to kill.

They were right. What they didn't know was that it was about to happen onstage.

8

At first everyone thought it was part of the song, a great new song, the rock hit of the decade. All the singers were screaming, some of them clawing to get off the stage. Others crawled and still others punched and pushed, and someone at a microhone cried out.

"Lord help us. Help us. Help."

The audience applauded as the center of the wooden stage began to sag and then with a sickening crack, it collapsed. Bodies fell into each other. Guitars and bones cracked in the onslaught. The center-stage singers were crushed under the load, smothered by the bodies of those who fell on top of them. It was a full minute before the audience realized this wasn't the best rock piece they had ever heard but a disaster.

Remo and Chiun saw immediately that the people were in trouble, not singing about it. Using the wires, they pulled Debbie and her guitar free and then dove into the center of the surging mass of bodies, lifting off rock stars, passing them up over the side of the stage. Those on the bottom could not be saved, but they managed to get the upper layers free so that doctors could get to those who were still alive at the bottom.

At the lower levels the bodies were slippery from the blood.

Some of the rock stars didn't realize what happened for the whole evening. One of them, with a punctured lung and enough cocaine coursing through his blood to numb the whole of southern California, only discovered he was injured when he tried to sing and nothing came out but blood.

Another with a broken hip, completely smashed on Quaaludes, thought she couldn't walk because this time she'd taken one pill too many. The idea made her giggle.

Debbie Pattie was furious that Remo and Chiun yanked her off the stage before she could get in front of the cameras.

"I hated all this anyway. All those other people sharing the attention. I was going crazy. I had withdrawals. I know others did, too."

One thing did make her feel better. At least it showed Remo that rock stars not only gave of their time and money but also of their blood.

"You can't say we're not saving now," said Debbie.

Remo ripped off the wires, and so did Chiun.

"Why do you use such sticky wires?" he asked.

"Hey, I'm talking to you. I said you can't say we're not saving now," said Debbie. "I mean, people are bleeding on that stage."

"I didn't say you didn't mean well," said Remo. "I just said jumping up and down and screaming 'Save' over and over doesn't mean anything. You're not saving people by dying, any more than you're saving people by screaming."

"That's singing," said Debbie.

"Whatever," said Remo. "Do you always use wires that stick?"

Debbie shrugged. She hired people for that. She honestly didn't know how a lightbulb worked, but when you made enough money, things just were supposed to work or you fired people.

"That's the difference between singers and nobodies," said Debbie.

Remo noticed that Rizzuto, who was standing at the front of the stage, had escaped the collapse of its center by simply jumping off. Being a good trial lawyer, he had the presence of mind to look for an open microphone. Finding one, he gave a last message to the people.

"Do not let them die in vain. Do not let them bleed in vain, everyone, you here and across the world, support change of venue for negligence. Please, I beg you in the name of humanity, the suffering humanity you see here, and the suffering you don't see which is even worse, write your congressmen. March in the streets. Barricade your courtrooms, Americans, because if the venue isn't changed to America, if it stays in Gupta where human life routinely suffers extermination by the powerful, then, friends, no humanity is safe. No mother is safe. No child is safe. No one is safe. You are not safe."

A stagehand wanted to borrow the microphone for a minute to get people in the rear to open a way for an ambulance. Rizzuto put his hand over the microphone.

"In a minute. In a minute, all right?"

"People are dying here, buddy. We got to get the ambulance."

"I said in a minute," said Rizzuto, and made one more appeal for the change of venue, this time telling the people in so many words that if they helped the class-action suit against International Carborundum & Phosphate, they would be saving their own air, their own water and, as Rizzuto put it with a trembling voice, "your own green, green grass of home."

Debbie Pattie saw Remo start to break away from her to get to Rizzuto.

"Hey, you're the luckiest man in the world. I'm ready to ball you. Let's go."

"Later," said Remo.

"Hey, I'm the most sexually desirable female in America," said Debbie.

"Sorry."

"Then I'll ball the old man, and he'll tell you what you missed. Everyone says I'm great in bed, everyone lucky enough."

"Fine," said Remo, easing his way through the stretchers and wounded. He knew that Debbie had as much chance of getting Chiun into bed as the pope. No, the pope would be easier. But if he told her that, she would keep bothering Chiun all night. Debbie Pattie wanted only one thing in life, it seemed. Whatever someone told her she couldn't have.

The thing that struck Remo about Rizzuto was that the man was only pressing the Gupta case. If each of those rock stars earned millions, and many of them would not be able to perform again, the size of the negligence suit would be awesome. And yet when Rizzuto dusted himself off, he went happily looking for what he called "action."

In Gupta, according to what Chiun found out, Rizzuto was right on the scene with a well-prepared case. Here, he walked past millions of dollars in liability, telling Remo that he thought he might know of a crap game in the hotel. Remo followed him, and that was exactly where Rizzuto went. There was a bigger negligence case on that one stage that evening than in all of Gupta, but Rizzuto ignored it.

And Palmer, Rizzuto & Schwartz, with a man already on the scene, made no move to get any part of it. In fact, it was one of the few really major cases that year that the firm didn't get.

Remo contacted Smith on a public phone. Somehow, and of course Remo did not know how, the line was secure the moment contact was made.

"Smitty. I don't know that this detective thing is getting anywhere. I can't figure out a lot of this. A lot of things don't make sense. What if we just gently hang Rizzuto out of a window somewhere and find out what really makes them tick, and then you move the evidence somewhere?"

"Holding someone out a window, Remo, is not evidence. Just find out how they're doing this, how they're causing these accidents, and I can get the evidence worked up from here for some prosecutor. We've got to destroy these guys in a courtroom. We've got to have the law appear as though it's taking care of its own. Legally we have to do what Chiun always wants us to do. Hang a head on the wall."

"I don't even know where the wall is in this case."

"Keep on it. And by the way, are you all right?"

"You mean that crazy business, or what you called that crazy business? Yeah. I'm fine. I haven't had a desire to do something decent for days. I just run around after people."

"I wasn't talking about that, Remo."

"What were you talking about?"

"To be honest, Remo, I don't know. Something is wrong. We're not getting the right readings from our sources. I backed everything off to the perimeters of the law firm's business and still our own system doesn't seem to make headway with them. We have a program that checks and analyzes every call they make. It's done automatically, even analyzed by the program itself. But every time their phone system connects to the Midwest it seems to suddenly go blank with an incredible amount of static."

"Like the system you use, Smitty?" asked Remo.

"Something like that, Remo. Except we're the only ones in the world who are supposed to have it. Or know how it works."

"So?"

"So, there's been an even stranger silence from that firm that I can't figure out. It's like that quiet in the jungle before a tiger strikes. Have you ever seen a cat stalk prey?"

"Maybe. I don't know. What are you getting at?"

"I think you're being stalked by someone or something."

"Why?"

"A hunch."

"Smitty, you don't play hunches. You don't even have hunches. In fact, I wonder if you have feelings sometimes. So how come you're coming up with hunches all of a sudden?"

"Because some of our systems don't seem to be working quite right. Granted, no one has penetrated us. But there is that strange sense of things like in the jungle when the birds stop singing."

"You're going crazy," said Remo.

"Watch yourself, all right?"

"Me and Chiun. Who do we have to be afraid of?"

"Didn't Chiun tell you?"

"Has he made contact with you?"

"I thought it would be a good safety precaution for me to keep in touch with you both."

"Because you think I'm crazy."

"Because I don't know what you're going to do. And it's a good thing I do have contact with Chiun because he thinks that for your own safety perhaps you should take off for a year or two and get out of the country, come back later when things are safer."

"He's hustling you. He wants us to get in on some business elsewhere. Nothing's bothering him. Is that where your hunch came from?"

"No. I'm warning you too. You're being stalked."

"You're both crazy," said Remo, and hung up.

In Folcroft Sanitarium, Harold W. Smith watched the computer screen taking readouts from a network across the nation. He wondered if he were losing his mental balance. After all, he really didn't play hunches and had never trusted them. Yet why did he have this feeling that not only was Remo being stalked, but by something he might ultimately be helpless against? Was the organization going to lose him after all these years? And if so, what would happen to the organization? It had come to rely on Remo and Chiun, perhaps too much.

Harold W. Smith did not like hunches because he couldn't analyze them. He could not explain in hard facts why his senses kept telling him Remo was now up against perhaps the one thing he couldn't handle. And there was no rational evidence for it. He had absolutely no idea of what that one thing was.

In the plush suite of Palmer, Rizzuto & Schwartz it was Palmer who almost threw a chair through the glass case enshrining their old storefront-office desk.

"What is that idiot Rizzuto doing? There are hundreds of millions of dollars to be made on that stage. Why is he talking about stinking little Gupta? Forget Gupta. Was Debbie Pattie hurt? If she were hurt we could earn double Dastrow's fee for Gupta."

"I think it was a real accident," said Schwartz.

"How do you know?"

"I don't know," said Schwartz. "I forget what they look like anymore."

"As good as Dastrow's," said Palmer.

"But they're more spontaneous, right?"

"Dastrow's are spontaneous. There's nothing more spontaneous than an air disaster. Dastrow's are very spontaneous. That's why we use him. The man is incredibly safe. But so what if this thing isn't his? That doesn't mean we can't clean up anyway. And Rizzuto's sitting on his goddamned hands out there."

"I never thought of rock concerts. What about the Academy Awards? Can you think of the value of an entire auditorium filled with producers, stars, directors, writers?" asked Schwartz. He rubbed his hands. He thought of having the auditorium collapse after the awards were given out so the winning victims would be worth more.

"You mean do an Academy Awards?" said Palmer. "Dastrow asks money up front."

"Give him a contingency fee like we work on."

"Writers aren't worth much," said Palmer. "We don't need the writers. We can do it without the writers. You don't get anything for writers."

"We can say the builders who negligently let that auditorium blow up or collapse or whatever Dastrow does with it, maybe poisons the air or something, we can say their lost lives are robbing our entire civilization of art."

"To say nothing of the studios' incomes."

"Yes, studios. The studios will be good."

Palmer dialed Dastrow's number and waited for the callback. It came about eveningtime as the sun set over the Pacific and Palmer, Rizzuto & Schwartz employees headed home on clogged freeways and Schwartz dozed.

"Listen. The accident in Chicago with the Gupta benefit gave me a great idea, Bob. A truly great idea. A wonderful idea. Instead of some accident with rock stars, what about the Academy Awards? We couldn't pay you up front, but perhaps a contingency-basis sort of thing . . . Bob, are you there, Bob?"

"I'm here," said Dastrow. "I'm just looking at something."

"What do you think?"

"About the Academy Awards?"

"That's right."

"I've already done an entertainment group," said Dastrow.

"You mean the Chicago rock disaster was yours?"

"Uh-huh."

"Are you working with someone else? Is that it? You think we're broke and you're working with someone else," Palmer moaned.

"No. You are the lawyers who work. You're the lawyers who work well with the sort of thing I do. You're the sort of lawyers I can always count on for this sort of work. You're fine."

"Then why did you do Chicago? We never discussed Chicago."

"I am trying to find out how something works."

"How what works?" screamed Palmer. Dastrow was always difficult in his own Midwest hayseed way. But this was impossible.

"What is going to destroy you if I don't."

"Thank you."

"I'm not doing it for you, Palmer. I've never done anything for you. Let's not be confused here. I do things for myself. If they get you, they're going to get me."

"They? Who are 'they'?"

"That's why I returned your call. I thought you might be able to tell me something about them. Most peculiar people I have ever seen. Absolutely strange. If you knew what I know, you would jump out of your windows right now."

"What do you know?"

"I know it's going to be fun, finding out what goes on with these two. I know I'm going to remove them from our lives forever. I know, dear Palmer, how things work."

And Dastrow hung up.

"What did he say?" asked Schwartz.

"He said no to a contingency-fee basis," said Palmer, "and Chicago was his, and no, he's not working with anyone else. You know, Arnold, I think that Midwest hoopie has found out how we work. After all these years, I think I realize he's been using us."

"Can we sue?"

"Go flash your Rolex," said Palmer. "If we were to sue Dastrow, the entire courtroom would turn against us. I guess I should have known that eventually he would have figured out how the legal system works. He figures out everything eventually. Could you imagine if his genius were somehow harnessed for good?"

"It is. He's making us money. We employ people. Our lawsuits help keep corporations more careful. By serving Palmer, Rizzuto & Schwartz, Robert Dastrow serves America in ways he may never fathom," said Schwartz.

"Do you honestly believe that nonsense?" asked Palmer.

"Just practicing," said Schwartz.

Robert Dastrow could not believe his calculations. And yet there they were. The Chicago disaster had worked to perfection. Without bodyguards, Debbie Pattie had to use those two who knew how Gupta worked but not how machines worked.

They, in turn, had responded to the disaster in front of them. Dastrow would have been satisfied with a quick leap back to safety. But instead, he got more body action than he could have hoped for.

He got tests of strength. Quickness. Balance. Nervous system, and of course blood-pressure levels and the intricate motor responses that made limbs work, all during the course of extreme stress.

Built into the power lines to Debbie Pattie's guitar were sensors to measure the body responses of those who held them. The lines were coated with thick, sticky conducting fluid to give better readings.

And the most amazing thing appeared to Robert Dastrow, like some strange jewel in an exotic clock that kept time as no other instrument might.

He held the white-and-green paper readouts in his hands, quivering with excitement in the large machine shop he had built underground at his Grand Island, Nebraska, estate. In those black numbers on the coarse paper, he saw evidence of balance that would be more appropriate to a cat than a human. He saw a nervous system respond with a strong, sure precision, as regular and dependable as radio waves from the center of the galaxy, and he saw awesome strength coupled with an unbelievably perfect muscular symmetry.

He glanced around the machine shop. There were more tools and instruments here than in most defense laboratories. The fluorescent lights glittered on the shiny instrument panels. Robert Dastrow felt his mouth go dry. He could think of only one thing seeing these figures, a poem by an Englishman.

"Tiger! Tiger! burning bright, in the forests of the night, what immortal hand or eye could frame thy fearful symmetry?"

Was that what William Blake was talking about? Dastrow had always thought the poet was talking about the basic force of the universe. Did life follow art?

They certainly didn't understand mechanical things. Where did their power come from? From this symmetry? Would they at last use it against Palmer, Rizzuto & Schwartz and in so doing inevitably reach Dastrow himself? And what had kept them from using this force against Rizzuto, the dramatic mouthpiece of the firm?

Was there something in these men that Dastrow had discovered in the workings of nature, and only dimly perceived in his calculations?

He looked at the numbers again. There was no question. As much as he would like to study them, he could no longer afford any such luxury. The numbers meant they had to die. But of course, killing them would pose a special problem. One just didn't plan on collapsing a roof, because these two might well walk away from it. They might walk away from anything. And when they walked away they would walk more quickly to their ultimate destination, which had to be Robert Dastrow himself. Why else would they have been making inquiries in Gupta?

Inquiries not as reporters, not as insurance men, not as factory personnel.

But inquiries about Palmer, Rizzuto & Schwartz. The two tigers in the night were coming for them, they were coming for all of them. The question was, as it had been from the beginning: Who were they, and how were they going to die? The difference was that now, after reading these reports on how they responded physically, Robert Dastrow had a very good idea.

Remo was on his way back to his hotel room when he saw a car pull up on the dark Chicago street. He could tell from the tense body positions of the men in the backseat of the car that they were going to fire something at him.

He moved fluidly in a lateral motion, and with their normally slow reflexes, the men in the backseat finally caught up with what was going on and jerked toward the direction Remo had been heading. By the time they completed their jerk, Remo was on line with the car and moving toward it, getting there by the time their guns rose.

He rammed them in their solar plexi and then let the two men recover while he chatted with the driver.

"Good night for killing, isn't it?" said Remo. The driver swallowed. He started to explain how he really didn't know the men in the backseat. He was just driving along and they happened to climb in. Why, were there guns in there? My goodness, there were indeed. The driver said he was leaving right now. He hated guns.

"Fine," said Remo. "You can go. But I'll keep your kneecaps here on the seat to make sure you'll return."

"Thanks, I guess I'll stay," said the driver.

"Who sent you?"

"You wouldn't believe it."

"I believe," said Remo, repeating an absolutely silly line from a movie he had seen. Some trainer was trying to teach a pupil some physical tricks and he had said that all the person had to do was believe in himself. It was the wrong word. When doing something tricky, belief could get you killed. It was the knowing that a person had to have, not believing one could do something. One had to know it, deep down in the bones and in every little muscle and nerve. And one only knew it when it was so.

"A voice. The voice said there was some money in a bag in a garbage can. The voice said pick it up. It was a down payment. There would be more, when we finished the job."

"Where would there be more?"

"He didn't say. But there was ten grand in the fuckin' bag and that's good enough for a hit, you know. Nothing personal."

When the two gunmen regained their breath, they told the same story. "Nothing personal," they repeated.

"Nothing personal," said Remo, and removed three felons from the population of Chicago with three precise strokes through the skulls into the frontal lobes. When he was done, three foreheads had nice, neat dents in them.

The car smelled of pine deodorizer coming from a statue on the windshield. Remo wiped the knuckle of his right forefinger on the plaid car seat and left.

Before he got two blocks a street gang known as the El Righteous Kanks informed him he was going to die by the knife. There were four of them, each wearing a T-shirt with some absurd symbol. They all

had stilettos as sharp as needles and as long as trow-
els. They were going to dig out his insides, they said.

It seemed that they hadn't bathed in weeks. Remo
moved upwind. One of the Kanks thought he was
trying to escape and blocked his way. He stood upwind. He did not stand upwind long because before
he knew what had happened his legs were flying
downwind with him attached to them. He collided
with a lamppost which did not yield, but his spine
did. He fell to the concrete sidewalk like a duffel with
the contents hanging out.

"Why do you announce what you're going to do?"
asked Remo. The El Righteous Kanks were black.
Remo imagined no white man had come into this
neighborhood alone before.

"Hey, man. We gotta have some fun. Ain't no one
bothered by bein' dead. He gotta know he gonna
die. We gon' downput' upside yo head."

"You're going to try to kill me, right?"

"No try, whitey. We do."

"Would you tell me if this is just some ordinary
run-of-the-mill mayhem which keeps this area unliv-
able? Or are you actually doing something construc-
tive like getting paid to kill me?"

"You don' do nuthin', whitey, but stan' there and
die. That's what whitey do. He here to die."

"I don't see any whites around here."

" 'Cause dey racists," said the leader of the El
Righteous Kanks. "But if we nail one o' dem racists,
we kill 'em all."

Remo took another line of reasoning. He applied
the apparent leader gently to the lamppost while the
other two attacked him. He pressed the other two
neatly against the same lamppost until their spines
cracked, and then suggested to the leader he would

continue the pattern. On the other hand, he might not continue the pattern if he could establish a dialogue.

"Anyone tell you to make a hit on me?"

"A voice. Crazy voice. Tol' us where money was. Tol' us there'd be mo'."

"That's it then, a voice?"

"Ah swear."

"I believe you," said Remo, and dropped the El Righteous Kank leader on top of the pile unharmed.

"By the way, where did you get the name Kank? Sounds like some sore."

"It be our black mystery, righteous Islamic."

"Somehow I doubt the accuracy of that," said Remo.

And before the hotel he avoided a thrown grenade, and this time he didn't even bother to ask who was behind it. It was, of course, a voice.

At the hotel, Remo found out that Debbie Pattie had found new bodyguards and this time Remo only moved through them so as not to injure them. He didn't want to have to carry her electronic gear anymore.

"Little father, something strange is happening. I am being— "

"Attacked by the gun and the knife and the bomb," said Chiun.

"Yeah. How did you know?"

"Look in the other room," said Chiun. "We are fools, I think. Here we are in this insanity called detective investigation, and you await our death."

"They didn't get us."

"They will," said Chiun.

"How can you say that? You know who we are."

"I know who we are. And soon they will know who

we are, if they do not already. And once they know
that, they can better kill us."

"Are you guys detectives?" asked Debbie. She had
switched to black rags instead of yellow and green
rags. Remo knew she had her own full-time seamstress
to sew the rags together. They were not taken out of
dime-store garbage pails but were actually manufac-
tured for her.

"No," said Remo. "We're just trying to find out
something."

"I thought you knew it all," she said. She winked
at Remo and nodded to the bedroom.

"Bodies in there," said Remo.

"Was that what Chiun was doing? Oh, he's neat.
He's beautiful. He's heavy. He's baddest."

"It is her way of attempting to explain perfection,
Remo. We must be tolerant of her," said Chiun.

"How are we going to be killed?" asked Remo. He
hadn't seen anything that would be a problem. The
problem was figuring out how to gather evidence
against the super shysters on the Coast, not getting
through the day alive.

Chiun raised a finger.

"There has been the gun, and that has failed,
correct?"

Remo nodded.

"And there has been the knife, and that has failed,
correct?"

Remo nodded. "And the grenade too, so what are
you talking about? No problem."

"If you fail, and fail, and fail, what does that mean?"
asked Chiun.

"It means you can't get bookings," said Debbie.

"I don't know," said Remo.

"It means that someday you will succeed. Remo,

the handmaiden of success is failure. There are only so many times a determined person can fail before he succeeds. And look at whom we face. Someone who understood how Gupta worked. I believe we are being tested. See what fails here, and see what fails there, and see what fails elsewhere, and all the while the failures are telling that person who we are and what we can do."

"I dunno," said Remo.

"On the one hand, Remo, we face someone who knows what he is doing while we have no idea what we are doing."

"Talk in Korean," said Remo.

"I'm old enough to hear anything you say," said Debbie. "And smarter than you think, too. Yeah."

But Chiun ignored her.

"We hunt these lawyers for proof for some judge. What sort of a country is it that an emperor cannot maintain order with a scaffold or sword? What is evidence but something someone else may believe? Is that what we hunt? We should hunt thundershowers for our purse and build walls from morning dew. We are made fools of. Do you not understand we do not belong here? If this were easy for us it would be right. But it is impossible."

"It's only impossible when you give up, little father. We will fail, and fail, and fail, and then succeed. What's good for our enemies is good for us."

"Unfortunately, Remo, when an assassin fails, he is usually dead for the trouble. Leave this crazy land and the crazy man Smith. Come with me to civilized people. Did you not feel the respect of India, the grandeur, the sanity, the beauty?"

"I saw a dirty river," said Remo.

"How American," said Chiun.

"I'm not giving up, little father. Every other country in the world has a tinpot dictator, where laws mean nothing. There's no difference between some despot and some glorious emperor," said Remo.

"That's what I am saying. This is the age of the despot, and here the glory of Sinanju wastes itself in foolishness beyond comprehension. We do not even serve a lunatic emperor like Smith any longer: we serve some poetry that you alone appear to believe in."

"Smith serves the same laws. And he's not insane. You just don't understand America."

"That's not the problem, Remo. You don't understand the world."

Debbie Pattie saw the two men fall into hostile silence. She did not understand a word they were saying, but she recognized a family fight when she saw one. She recognized two people thinking each other stubborn and unreasonable.

She also recognized a chance to make her point.

"Look," she said. "I know you think I don't know what I'm doing with all these crazy rags and the weird colors and downright junk I dress in, but I do. Nobody ever paid a million dollars for Beethoven's Fifth. This is what makes money. And so this is what I do, understand? I mean, I couldn't be a heavyweight boxer, right? I couldn't really be an opera star, because I don't have a voice that would carry past the first row. So I did what I could do without any talent. And I did all right, too. I'm famous and I'm rich, and that ain't bad if all you can do is yell and dress bad."

Debbie paused. Her voice lowered, and they could hear the tears beginning.

"So what I'm saying, fellas, is would you please be

a little bit understanding of someone who works different from you? Huh? How about it? A little human understanding, Remo?"

"No," said Remo. "I don't believe in it, and Chiun believes in it even less."

"Okay, you poor moneyless jerk, I'll show you I have smarts. I'm going to show you where every penny of that Save benefit went. I'm going to show you you're wrong. You're wrong about everything. Because whether you know it or not, I love you, you big ape," she said to Remo.

"I didn't know that," said Remo.

"Well, I do," said Debbie, her tears making a rainbow stream through her multicolored makeup.

Remo shrugged. It didn't make any difference to him. Chiun, of course, was not surprised. The girl was the epitome of bad taste.

For Chiun, only one thing really mattered. He knew that if something did not change soon, he might lose Remo. And this mattered much, much more than he would ever let Remo know.

9

During World War II, when defense planners identified the seven most likely targets for the maximum possible damage to the United States, the Grand Booree Dam on the Colorado River rated right behind the destruction of the capital itself.

The project was immense. Not since the pyramids had mankind produced anything so massive. At its base the dam was almost a half-mile wide. In a perfect awesome slope of reinforced concrete it rose to the top of the canyon, almost as high as it was wide.

Major U.S. highways were built just to transport material to the construction site. A rail line for the concrete alone was built along the upper ridge of the Booree Canyon. Enough concrete was used in the making of Grand Booree to build twelve cities.

And behind its massive wall, a lake formed of such size that if the government chose, it could lose a fleet of battleships there. Homes and cities rose around the lake. And it was this lake that gave defense planners such nightmares.

If an enemy chose to destroy the dam, the force of the unleashed waters cascading down the canyon

would obliterate everything under a wall of water
that would shame any tidal wave yet recorded.

It was a nightmare that had moved this dam in
Colorado right up the list of most vulnerable targets.
It stayed there until a military officer took one look
at the project and asked quite simply, "How would
they destroy it?"

He calculated that for Japan or Germany to put
even a single hole in the Grand Booree they would
need a round-the-clock fleet of heavy bombers pound-
ing the dam for three weeks straight. Even if Germany or Japan could mount such an extensive air
bombardment, penetrating formidable coastal defenses, they would certainly not bother to do it to
flood a few cities in Colorado.

What about a saboteur's bomb? the officer was
asked.

"In terms of known explosives, to put a hole into
that mass of concrete would require the national
production of dynamite for August and September,
or roughly four full trainloads."

There was no way any saboteur could sneak in
enough explosives to do damage to the Grand Booree.
Nevertheless, the very thought of what could happen
if the lake ever let loose on the valley downriver was
enough to force the government to station antiair-
craft batteries around its perimeter and limit access
to it all through the war. The government felt it just
had to do something, even if something was absolutely not needed.

The residents of the valley numbered twenty-seven
people, most of them guides who could easily have
been trucked away. But the Grand Booree was an
object of national pride; its lake was as important a
public symbol as the Statue of Liberty.

The word from the top had been that Grand Booree was too big to be ignored. Robert Dastrow knew this was still government thinking, as he informed Nathan Palmer that he was about to do a freebie for Palmer, Rizzuto & Schwartz.

"Never mind why I'm doing this. You can pay me later. Just get your young lawyers into the Booree Canyon to warn the people that the Booree was badly built and might go any day now."

"The Booree? How are you going to do the Booree?"

"Never mind. Just get your people out there. Make a lot of noise. Attract attention. Do whatever you have to do to make sure people sit up and take notice."

"But we usually don't want to be noticed."

"This time, you do," said Dastrow. "Be sure you make noise now. We're fishing, so to speak."

When the young spokesmen for Palmer, Rizzuto & Schwartz came into the canyon to warn the few residents there, they were greeted with derision. The governor of the state went on television to laugh at the crazy lawyers. It became a popular joke that Palmer, Rizzuto & Schwartz had run out of disasters to chase, so instead they were hallucinating them. Palmer worried that the dam wouldn't go and their investment would be lost. Schwartz worried that the dam would go and for the first time Dastrow would have them linked as possible suspects in its destruction. Rizzuto worried about filling an inside straight with two men he met on an airplane, and in Folcroft Sanitarium Harold W. Smith took the threat of the Grand Booree more seriously than anyone else in the country.

It was a threat he couldn't possibly resist. Palmer, Rizzuto & Schwartz had made a mistake. They were, for the first time, establishing a trail right to themselves.

At their first check-in he ordered Remo and Chiun into Booree, Colorado. As soon as Remo nailed the evidence he was to inform Smith, and Smith would move it through normal channels back into the justice system, where the law firm of Palmer, Rizzuto & Schwartz, to say nothing of Messrs. Palmer, Rizzuto, and Schwartz individually, could at last pay for their crimes.

"Well, we finally got 'em now, little father," said Remo as he made sure the fourteen steamer trunks with the kimonos for all occasions were packed and organized for the bellboys to wrestle into the elevator.

"We have nothing. We have insanity. Even the girl dressed in rags made more sense than you. She understood money. She understood the purpose of work is to make money. You don't even understand what you do things for anymore."

"No, it's you who don't understand," said Remo.

"This is childish," said Chiun. "It could go on for days, you saying I don't understand and I saying you don't understand. Let us just let the subject drop."

"Okay," said Remo.

"Because you don't understand," said Chiun, following the trunks out the door.

On the plane to Denver Chiun opened the magazines, pointing out stories about how people worked for money. Everyone else in the world worked for money but Chiun's lunatic protégé.

"I thought we were going to let the subject drop," said Remo.

"I am dropping it."

"Then do it."

"Done. Why should I want to talk about how you are breaking my heart?" said Chiun.

"If I don't do exactly what you want, exactly when you want, your heart is broken."

"I hardly consider your betrayal of everything we stand for something so petty as 'not exactly what I want.' "

"This may come as a surprise to you, but guilt does not work with me," said Remo.

"Why should my suffering ever bother you? What have I done for you, other than teach you everything you know from breathing to movement? What should I expect in return for this, for the best years of my life?"

Several people in the first-class section were now listening to Chiun. A young girl thought Remo was awful. A middle-aged man kept casting angry glances at him. A flight attendant comforted Chiun. A woman named Goldstein was taking notes, commenting that Chiun was an absolute master of communication.

"See, even she knows," said Chiun.

"She probably meant 'master at communicating guilt,' " said Remo. "I don't care how much other people make. I don't care how much glory other Masters have brought to Sinanju. I do my job. I like my job. It's my job and I'm happy with it, dammit. Case closed. Good night. I'm taking a nap."

"Sleep well," said Chiun.

"Thank you," said Remo angrily.

"On the tears of one who loves you," said Chiun, who then dozed off contentedly while Remo fumed.

"I never win with him," said Remo.

"Why should you?" said a flight attendant.

On the drive from Denver to Grand Booree, Chiun decided he was going to let Remo find his own way. He would no longer berate him for what he felt he had to do.

Indeed, Chiun was most pleasant during the drive, saying how much he respected and liked Remo.

"You have become a Master, something not always possible even for those of Sinanju. You are truly a good son in so many ways. Your loyalty to most of that which is Sinanju has impressed me over the years. I have felt pride in your glory. For your glory, Remo, is the glory of Sinanju."

Remo waited for the other shoe to drop. He recognized a setup when he heard one. But the other shoe didn't drop. Chiun just repeated how much he respected and loved Remo. That Remo was better than anyone from Sinanju except, of course, Chiun, which was why Chiun had stayed so long. If Remo weren't wonderful, Chiun would not have wasted a minute beyond the initial time paid for by Smith for the training.

"Perhaps you do not even know the moment I knew you were someone special, even in white skin."

Remo cast a quick glance at Chiun. The voice was soft, the hands were complacently at rest in the lap of the traveling kimono. The face was benign. This was when Chiun was most dangerous.

Remo did not venture an answer.

"It was when I saw a star in your eye. It is greatness that comes from a mystery. Is it the blood of birth? Is it the forge that tempers a soul? Is it the soul itself? Even Masters of Sinanju do not know this. But you had it, my son," said Chiun.

Remo did not answer. He drove in silence, but Chiun did not attack him once. In the small town of Booree, alongside the lake above the massive dam, Remo finally exploded.

"All right. I give up. Why are you being so nice to me?"

"Because you are going to die, Remo," said Chiun, and he said it so plainly that Remo believed him. This was not a game. It was not a manipulation.

Remo thought for a while. He finally said, "Not without a fight, little father."

"May the Masters of Sinanju look down on me with pity. I train a Master of Sinanju who believes that second place in a fight to the death is all right provided he performs well."

In Booree the laughter among the people had suddenly changed. People were now talking about how much less their homes would be worth if they bordered a big pit instead of Lake Booree. Every few moments people cast worried glances at the top of the dam. And Remo could feel what was going on. Through the reddish clay of what had once been the top of a canyon and was now the lake's shore, Remo could feel a slight rhythmic tremble every few moments.

The birds winging over the dam sensed the danger, cawing strange calls. Remo sniffed the water and the air: it smelled of impending disaster.

" 'Course you can't tell a thing from here," said an old-timer with a sun-grizzled neck and a face as worn as a leather saddle. "But engineers say the Grand Booree, she's beginnin' to tremble. Vibrations like. Slow now but they're pickin' up. Those lawyer fellas sure are smart 'bout what's happenin'. They said it would. Said the government was negligent when they built her. Nobody ever thought that, but it sure looks like it's true."

"Who says the Booree is going to go?"

"Engineers. Came in to check once those lawyer fellas got around sayin' so. If you own property here, better sign up with them. They sure know what they're talkin' 'bout. Chief engineer wonders how they could've figured it out."

"Where is he?"

"Over at Grand Booree. But better not go there. It's a danger zone now."

Before Remo left for the dam itself, Chiun gave him an order.

"Forget all our troubles. Forget everything but what your body has been taught. Listen to your body. It has learned everything it needs."

"Thank you," said Remo.

"You will survive," said Chiun.

"Yes. I will survive." And then there was a long silence, broken only when Chiun turned away to let his thoughts and being quiet and focus on the center of the universe.

At the dam Calvin Rutherford was giving orders. He wore a plastic safety helmet, and his white shirt pocket contained a plastic case filled with pencils and pens. His face was ashen, and every few moments he sighed in frustration and rage, feeling more helpless by the moment.

When he saw Remo he ordered him off the dam.

"This is no place to be," said Rutherford.

"I'm safer than you are. Do you know how this happened?"

"You from the government?"

"Yeah. Who the hell else would be interested?"

"Reporters," said Rutherford. "But what the hell. I've already told them. I'll tell you. Don't care who sues us. This is a disgrace. The damned engineers made a mistake."

"After all these years?"

"Hell, the mistake didn't happen now. It's just

showing up now. I'll take you down to see for yourself."

Inside the dam Remo could feel its mass. He sensed the hugeness of this man-made mountain. He felt the awesome weight of the water in Lake Booree, and sensed the vibrations through the elevator that had brought him and Engineer Rutherford twenty stories down into the bowels of the Grand Booree.

They walked through a half-mile of internal piping that Rutherford explained in detail and Remo did not understand at all.

"A dam, any dam, has got to have its sluices working. You've got to let the water out below, because if it comes out over the top, it'll be useless for energy and eventually will wear down the surface of the dam, grind it down just like waterfalls do to the stone they fall on, understand?"

Remo nodded. He thought he understood.

"So the sluices are important. It's what we run the turbines with. Water pressure pushes the blades and we create electricity. The Grand Booree supplies much of Colorado. Okay?"

"Gotcha," said Remo.

"Now, understanding the turbines, you've got to understand vibrations. Soldiers break step when they walk across a bridge because otherwise the vibrations would set the bridge to rocking. What we have here are not cables, but masses of concrete. The very mass has picked up the vibrations from turbines synchronized in such a way as to turn this whole damned incredible mass of concrete into a pane of window glass that'll crack when the vibrations get strong enough."

"So where was the negligence?" asked Remo.

"You sound like a lawyer."

"I'm trying to catch lawyers."

"The negligence is that not only did we fail to perceive the effect of synchronized vibrations but we built the turbines in such a way as to be able to run them in only one direction."

"What's wrong with that?"

"If we could get them reversed to create a counter vibration, which would be diametrically opposed to the one that is gathering momentum now, we could stop the vibrations perfectly."

"Well, why not just shut down the turbines? Won't that stop everything from shaking?"

"No, it's too late for that. Other than reversing the turbines, the only solution's a construction one. We're working on it now."

"So what's the problem?"

"The problem is we have to reconstruct the sluices at the entrance point. In other words, we have to do it from underwater at lakeside. We've got divers there now."

"Good," said Remo.

"Not so good," said Rutherford. "The desilting of the bottom near the sluices is due this month. The whole area is so heavy with silt from the bottom of the lake that our diving gear keeps getting fouled. If only this had happened a month from now we would be okay. Divers are just having no luck in the goo, and if we don't fix those sluice entrances pretty soon, the divers, the diving barge, and everything is going to go along with the dam."

Remo saw the giant turbines set with metal bolts twice the size of a man.

"Pretty soon," said Rutherford, "you're going to be able to feel the vibrations. Then they'll continue to build on themselves until . . . boom!"

"How much time do we have?"

"A half hour till I clear everyone out of here."

On top of the dam Remo saw a large sign calling the Grand Booree "America's Pride." It was built during the Depression when a president had to give hope to a nation. It was a symbol as much as it was a stunning technical achievement to keep a river in check and provide electricity.

Men on the barge were signaling Rutherford with their hands. He had a walkie-talkie on his hip. He pulled out its antennas.

Remo heard the voice crackle across the airwaves.

"Too much silt. Can't work in that much silt. That's what's fouling the diving gear," came the voice.

"I can work in silt," said Remo.

"You a diver?"

"Sure," said Remo.

"I thought you were an investigator for the government."

"Used to be a frogman," Remo lied.

He wasn't going to let America's Pride go under and he was grateful that Chiun wasn't there to see him do it.

"Explain to me again what has to be done," said Remo, taking over a diving suit on the barge. The other divers were warning against trying.

"You'll be buried alive. You can't get down there. It's like a big blanket clinging to your gear. There's nothing but death down there."

"Shh," said Remo. "I'm trying to understand how that sluice works."

"It's not the sluice that's a problem. It's the silt," said Rutherford. "If you really want to see something that'll make it simple for you, read this."

He took a flier out of his rear pocket. It had been

folded several times. Over a pale gray sketch of the Grand Booree was a message to concerned citizens. It came from the law firm of Palmer, Rizzuto & Schwartz. It decried an age when the lives of people were of little concern to a government bent on aggrandizing its image. It did not matter that the aggrandizing had been done a half-century before. The problem was coming to a crisis point now.

Because the government had rushed ahead without testing the massive structure, it was vulnerable to vibrations. Just when the vibrations would come, the law firm did not know. Hopefully, the flier stated, this would never happen. But should the vibrations occur, and if the vibrations should be caused by a buildup of silt at the sluices, the only way to stop them was to reach the sluices from the lake side of the dam. And that meant diving. But because of an engineering oversight, the flier continued, the sluice entrances were below, not above, the sluices. And this underwater area was now almost completely obstructed by silt.

"Absolutely simple," said Rutherford. "If we had put the openings above instead of below, we could get in."

"Why didn't you?"

"Why didn't I? Hell. I wasn't born then, and whoever thought there would be a problem today back then?"

"So I have to get in from below. Okay," said Remo. He stepped into the diving suit, feeling the rubber wet and cold against his skin. He let his mouth breathe for him and then put on the diving mask and tanks.

He ignored the offer of fins and jumped overboard. On deck the crew noticed something peculiar.

"Hey, there's no bubbles coming from him."

"I didn't think he looked like he knew what he was doing," said one diver.

They waited five minutes, and when they didn't see a bubble they declared him dead. Atop the dam, the sign declaring the Grand Booree to be America's Pride quivered and fell.

"Vibrations are reaching maximum. It's gonna go. No point waiting for that guy. He's dead. Let's get out of here," said Rutherford.

"Maybe he's not dead," said one of the divers.

"And maybe he don't have to breathe either. Let's get out of here. You can even see the vibrations now."

Not only had the sign fallen, but across the vast dark lake little waves appeared like the ridges of a giant washboard. Along the shore the trees quivered and dropped their leaves, and down in the darkness of the silt Remo Williams searched for the opening.

As soon as he was out of sight, Remo took off the mask and rubber suit, allowing his skin to acquaint itself with the cool water. It was not that he stopped breathing. He would never completely stop breathing. Instead he used the technique borrowed from the Indian fakirs, who buried themselves alive for hours at a time. By slowing the rhythms of his body he required less oxygen than an unconscious person. Yet his nervous system functioned at peak efficiency. He knew that his muscles suffered from the reduced oxygen absorption, but it wasn't muscles that made Remo a Master of Sinanju.

The problem was finding the opening in the silt. At the top, it felt like some strange oil on his body, but farther down it became densely packed like un-set concrete. Even farther down it was like moving through settled clay: hard, dense, packed clay. Remo kept his eyes shut and moved along the cement base, pausing every few moments to let his palms press open-fingered against the coarse concrete, trying to distinguish the normal vibrations of the water going through the sluice from those which seized the concrete mass and were obviously growing.

The plan was to create an opening through an entranceway beneath the sluice. Remo got there and found the metal plate Rutherford had predicted would be there. It had to be moved in one direction or another, and Remo couldn't figure out which. As the vibrations forced him back, Remo cut through the silt once again to reach the plate. Something had to be done with the plate. He sensed the dam might go at any second. Taking the plate in his hands, Remo did what he did to old television sets, whose workings he also didn't understand. He gave it a kick. The only difference was that nowadays he kicked televisions very, very gently.

The kick was backed up by the weight of all the damned-up water guided by the rhythms of Remo's body. His foot went through the metal like a torpedo. With a muffled sucking sound, the silt was pulled through the hole, creating a rhythm of its own. The turbines stopped, clogged by mud. The dam quivered and the vibrations ceased. But Remo saw too late that it was a trap. Someone had expected him.

The only thing in the narrow sluiceway between the open air above and the lake itself was Remo Williams—and a small, carefully placed explosive device. When the explosive charge detonated, he was propelled by the force of tons of lake water, shooting out through the sluice like a pea through a straw, the mud behind him and the rocky riverbed below.

Blinded momentarily by the mud, he almost did
the one thing that could get him killed: he started to
tighten his muscles against the impact. But his muscles knew better. They had been trained too well by
Chiun, and so instead he stretched out like a long
strand of silk. As he let the mud and water wash over
him, becoming one with the lake and the riverbed,
he let the mud behind him absorb the impact of the
explosion.

He moved down the shallow river for about a
quarter of a mile and then climbed up the bank.
Behind him the dam disgorged mud and water, but
not so much as to cause flooding. The dam had
stopped vibrating. America's pride had held.

Along the lakeshore, Calvin Rutherford and the
other engineers were reading their meters and cheer-
ing. The sluice could be closed and the smashed
turbine would be replaced. As a side benefit the
powerful current was even desilting the lake, carrying tons downriver. At this rate, they would probably not have to dredge.

When Chiun saw Remo walk up the road covered
with mud, he felt joy that Remo was alive. In an
instant he knew his joy was to be fleeting.

Remo walked into the motel room with a big grin.

"Well, here I am, little father. Alive."

"So far," said Chiun. "But I have come to the
conclusion we have only one chance."

"What's the one chance?" asked Remo as he headed
for the shower to wash off the mud. Even his pores
had breathed it in under the pressure of the water,
and his body had to breathe it out again.

"We must join this Palmer, Rizzuto, and Schwartz,
who we are not allowed to kill, and eliminate Smith for
them. That is our only way. And it is righteous."

"How is betrayal righteous?" said Remo, stepping into the shower. He didn't use soap, because soap, which actually burned off dirt with lye, left its fatty residue still burning his skin.

"It is not we who are betraying the mad emperor Smith, but he who is betraying us."

"I thought we worked for him."

"Assassins are not used as targets. In decent civilized lands, like India, people appreciate a great assassin for what he is. In America he is turned into a palace guard, some local official who investigates things. A catcher of thieves."

"Detective," said Remo.

"That," said Chiun.

"I used to be a cop," said Remo.

"All this training, the awesomeness of Sinanju, and you are still a cop."

Remo paused before turning on the water.

"Little father. I have not dishonored Sinanju. I have not learned nothing. But you did teach it to an American. So I am an American and I am Sinanju."

"One cannot be both Sinanju and American, two things at the same time. This is impossible."

"But I am."

"Then get rid of the lesser one, or die."

"Okay," said Remo. "I'll get rid of Sinanju."

"You can't," said Chiun. "I have trained you. You are Sinanju. You can no more rid yourself of Sinanju than a cloud can forfeit its air, or the sun its light, or the river its water."

"So I'll stay stuck."

"You could try ridding yourself of being American. There are two hundred million of those. The world will not mourn the loss of one."

"You know that's not possible either."

"Then, my son, you are dead, unless we kill Smith. There is precedence for it. Good precedence."

"You mean a tale of Sinanju? Which one was it? The Great Wang, and the Ming emperor? Let's see, he pointed out that an assassin never lost a king, so that certainly wouldn't be the Great Wang, or even the Lesser Wang, who did only one assignment, which wasn't all that important anyway. Then we have the middle period when the House of Sinanju worked Asia heavily. Could it have been the gateway to the West, when we served Rome and the caesars who never took our advice? No, I think we worked for Livia, except she was a chronic do-it-yourselfer, if I remember correctly, poisoning people. Then there was the later Western period of Ivan the Righteous, whom the rest of the world called the Terrible but whom we knew as a man of honor who paid on time."

"Do not mock the glory of Sinanju! You know perfectly well it was Sayak, during the middle period, a time of prosperity and peace and honor."

"Wasn't that something to do with a love affair? Some tawdry thing a private detective in America might handle? An unfaithful spouse?"

"Like a typical American, you remembered the dirt and missed the point. If you remembered the point we would happily join with this firm of lawyers right now and kill Smith. This already has good, solid precedent in the lesson of Master Sayak, who, when faced with death, when faced with a bitter, bitter choice, made the right choice and continued the line of Masters of Sinanju. For there is one thing a Master must know before all else: to continue the line he must not allow himself to be killed. There is nothing any more noble in death than there is something noble about rotting fruit. One does whatever possible to delay that inevitability. Fruit and life."

Chiun folded his hands in his kimono and shut his eyes. Remo had learned well the tale of Master Sayak from the histories of Sinanju. As he thought about it, he returned to his shower, turning on both the hot and cold water slowly, until a warm, comfortable mixture streamed over his body. Strategically, Chiun was not all that wrong. The tale of Master Sayak applied all too well to this situation.

The more Remo thought about it, the more troubled he became. It appeared Chiun might be right. Killing Smith might be the only way to survive. But did Remo want to survive at that price? What was life worth?

He wasn't born in Sinanju, where life was a struggle, where pushing it on to old age was a major triumph, especially for an assassin.

And he was not just a killer. He was Sinanju just as much as he was American, but not more. He let the warm water splash against his face and received the water now as a gentle stream, just as he had received it as an immense force shooting him through the sluice.

He had been given Sinanju, and it was a trust for the future as much as it was a tool for the present. He let the water touch his body, become one with his body, and tried to forget the tale of Master Sayak.

10

From the histories of Sinanju: "The Tale of Master Sayak and the Emperor's Concubine":

And it came to pass, during the masterhood of Sayak, that an emperor of a kingdom west of the middle kingdom of China, on his throne in Rhatpur north of the populated city of Delhi, suffered an affront to his life of such skill and daring that he realized no guards would keep him alive, no soldiers could stay the dagger now aimed at his imperial heart.

And beseeching Sinanju he sent a courier with a message. "O Master, my empire is held in the grip of a murderer's blade. None of my ministers or captains know how to help. No shield will prove sufficient. Only Sinanju and its glory can sustain my kingdom. Ask but the price and it will be delivered unto you."

Now, Sayak knew Emperor Mujjipur was the grandson of Emperor Shivrat, who paid well and promptly to the House of Sinanju when seizing the throne from his brother, and Sayak knew that blood often ran true. And the honor of a grandfather was often passed through the blood to the grandson.

But Sayak had made one mistake. Being Sinanju, he assumed that the problems of a soldier or a minister would not be problems for a Master of Sinanju. So he did not ask about the problems. But when there is a thunderstorm, the wagons of Master and soldier, Master and peasant, Master and courtesan, are all stuck in the same mud.

And when Sayak presented himself to Emperor Mujjipur in the summer palace of Rhatpur, the emperor gave to him a freedom few emperors would have allowed.

"To protect my royal life you are given fiat to kill whoever in my kingdom threatens that royal life," said Emperor Mujjipur. "Only one person may you never kill. Only one person's life must at all cost be spared, no matter what the provocation, and that is my beloved concubine, Hareen. No harm may come to her under any circumstance."

Now, Emperor Mujjipur was an old man, in his middle fifties, and his girth was wide, his breathing heavy, and his life hanging by a thread. And yet in that age men often delude themselves about love, and like boys again believe that whoever they happen to love at the moment is a gem beyond compare. So Sayak did not think this announced protection as anything unusual.

Besides, in these situations, such announcements are irrelevant. If Emperor Mujjipur had placed such a prohibition on a son or a cousin, then that might have posed a problem, because in these matters, the one who benefits from the removal of the emperor, the one likely to inherit the throne, is usually the one who seeks the ruler's death.

More significantly, though he had granted his concubine her protection, he had failed to put the empress under that protection. For if he loved this concubine Hareen so much, the queen, out of anger, might possibly have sought Mujjipur's death. Sayak understood the purpose of royal marriages is not sexual but political. Yet he was aware that some empresses felt themselves lovers as well as consorts of their mates. As a Sinanju saying went, all the best planning in the world could get out of hand in a lover's bed.

Yet this was not the case with the empress, who only laughed when Master Sayak respectfully asked her of her life at court, hoping to find the source of her troubles.

"We are all doomed because of the emperor's foolishness—me second, assassin, and you first," she said, and would explain no more.

Sayak knew there was only one way to avert danger and that was, of course, to stop it at the source, which was most simply done at the moment the danger struck. For the most deadly point is also the most vulnerable point.

And it came to pass that the assassin who had attempted twice before to steal the life of Mujjipur sent another deadly hand against the emperor.

He was a common strangler of some skills and some strength, but one of insufficient power. Sayak easily took the strangler's rope and put it about the strangler's neck, turning it slowly so that the face purpled and the teeth bared as the strangler struggled for breath, a move designed to injure the mind more than the body. The strangler would know for the first time, firsthand, the suffering he wrought and fear it.

Naturally it worked, and the strangler said he had been hired by a young captain in the palace quarters of the concubine Hareen. And keeping his promise, Sayak did not put the strangler to death with the rope, but dispatched him with a certain speed that would be welcomed by any of the dying. For it is not the purpose of Sinanju to cause pain. Pain for pain's sake alone is a waste and the mark of a sloppy assassin, and Sinanju would never allow that.

Knowing the injunction, Sayak formally asked the emperor for permission merely to enter Hareen's quarters.

"I honor this beauty so much that I allowed as how her quarters were like her kingdom. You must ask her permission," said the emperor.

But Sayak saw a danger. "Oh gracious Emperor, ruler from the throne at Rhatpur, light unto your subjects, the land you do not control in your own kingdom is land set against you. And land set against you is a danger."

"Sayak, from Sinanju in the Koreas, you have not seen her soft skin, or her eyes as bright as all the mornings of all the suns of all the universes. You have not seen her smile, or receive your body with her gentle love. You cannot know the rapture of this heavenly creature."

And so the answer was no. And Hareen refused even to see Master Sayak. Shortly thereafter there came five men with spears to take the life of the emperor, and these five did Sayak dispatch, but not before these five did again point the finger to the young captain in the quarters of the beautiful Hareen.

And again Mujjipur forbade entrance, saying he had mentioned this to Hareen and that it had brought her to tears.

The next killers came in a band of twenty, with arrows and slings and all manner of death in their hands, and Sayak through Sinanju prevailed, although this time the arrows were close, and the missiles closer, and he knew that while he could defeat the next in all probability and the one after that in all probability, sooner or later even a Master of Sinanju would suffer loss if all he did was sit as a target, like the emperor.

And he told this to Mujjipur, saying the emperor must take back his word to the concubine Hareen.

An enraged Mujjipur called Sayak a lesser Master of Sinanju.

"All I ask is that you protect my life without harming my one blessed relief in a burdensome kingdom, and you say you have failed. Since when does Sinanju fail?"

Now, knowing one should never call an emperor fool, Sayak accepted the rebuke and promptly entered the quarters of the beautiful Hareen.

She was in the arms of the captain who had sent the killers one after another against her emperor. She told Sayak she would have him executed for violating the sanctity of her quarters. She told him her Mujjipur would never allow his ears to hear of infidelity. She told Sayak to leave the throne at Rhatpur and return like a dog to the kennels of Sinanju.

Sayak heard her noise, but saw her predicament. This was a girl in love, for otherwise she would have accepted the favors of the emperor and grown rich and comfortable, a noble purpose for a courtesan, for in fact that would mean that her family and village would be secure from want. Sayak could appreciate this, for he provided the same security for his poor village, Sinanju, on the rocky slopes of the West Korea Bay.

Seeing Hareen lying on the multicolored pillows with soft silk cascading about her and her lover in her arms, Sayak saw she had made an improper move for a courtesan. For she did not seek the crown, but someone else, and of course it was he who controlled the beautiful Hareen, the captain of her guard, the man who held her now.

And with the inimitable grace of Sinanju, Sayak did move upon the multicolored pillows and snuff out the life of the captain, even while the beautiful Hareen screamed of murder, screamed of treachery, screamed she would see Sayak's death, no matter what the cost.

Using the force of her anger, Sayak let the anger work around her body in traditional ways, as he prepared to move her from the tension of anger quite naturally into relaxation with common touching and breathing techniques of the first level of Sinanju, and then up to sexual tension. At the height of her transformed energy, he took her, bringing her to an orgasm of peak intensity.

Since it was her body and not her mind that craved the captain, it was her body now that told her she loved Sayak.

And indeed, this beautiful girl who was no more than sixteen offered some attraction for Sayak, for even though Masters of Sinanju are at one with their bodies, they are still men. And she was a most beautiful being, rounded perfectly in all the places that were to be rounded, and thinned in all the places that were to be thinned, and smelling too of lilacs and roses and all the fragrances of a thousand gardens on her perfect skin.

But Sayak was Sinanju, and abiding by his responsibility he told her that first she must order the death of the emperor, order it from Sinanju, as a service. She did this readily, as she had gone along with the now dead captain.

That night Sayak sent the Emperor Mujjipur from a peaceful sleep into the deepest sleep for which there was no morning.

And by so doing, Sayak stilled the one voice that would accuse Sinanju of failure, though it had been the emperor's failure all along. But one could not be too careful about evil words from clients. Mujjipur had no right to defame Sinanju for his own faults, and thus justice was done, a necessary justice because Sayak knew that sooner or later even he would have succumbed.

Now Hareen did not want her new lover Sayak to leave, offering him instead the throne at Rhatpur.

But Sayak said, and it should be remembered by every Master unto the ages when all men leave the earth and assassins are no longer needed, "Beautiful Hareen, you offer me the throne at Rhatpur. But look now, a thousand years ago there was a kingdom here which you do not remember, and a thousand years from now, there will be a kingdom here which will not remember the throne of Rhatpur. But a thousand years ago, there was Sinanju, and a thousand years hence there will be Sinanju."

And the lesson from this tale of Master Sayak was that an emperor who foolishly does not allow his assassin to do his job has not hired him. But he who will let an assassin be what he should be, that one is the rightful employer.

Thus it was written in the histories of Sinanju that there was a time when a Master owed to Sinanju the correct move in seeking the right employer for the awesome talents and power of Sinanju.

Millennia later, in a motel shower alongside Lake Booree in Colorado, getting the mud out of his body pores, Remo remembered the tale of Master Sayak and knew Chiun was right. He had almost died in saving that dam. He finished washing, dried off, and put on his slacks and T-shirt. He could travel with all his clothes in a briefcase. He had never gotten into wearing kimonos as Chiun had tried to have him do. He didn't like them, and Chiun attributed this bad habit to early training which could not be broken.

Remo paused before the meditating Chiun.

"I could never get myself to work for Palmer, Rizzuto & Schwartz," he said.

And Chiun knew Remo had been thinking properly.

"We can then leave. Insane Smith would never say we had failed; he is obsessed with keeping our glory hidden. Why would he not do the same for our shame?"

"I guess you're right, little father," said Remo. "I guess it has come to that."

In Chicago, Debbie Pattie had made a fantastic discovery. She had launched her team of accountants into the books of the Save concert. Out of the twenty-five million dollars raised, her accountants tracked down exactly what was reaching Gupta, India. It was sent in an express package two feet wide and one foot tall. Exactly thirty-five dollars' worth of Band-Aids.

Enraged in large part because the man she wanted, Remo, had been right, and more important, didn't want to go to bed with her, Debbie immediately set out to raise a cry in the land about the fraud.

She contacted the leading rock singers of the Save concert. One of them, who yelled about being an American and wore a bandanna around his head, showing lots of sweat and muscle, was Barry Horowitz, sometimes called The Man.

He was strong. He was radical. He was concerned.

"Barry, this is Debbie Pattie. I found out something horrible. Do you know that for all our work we are only sending thirty-five dollars in Band-Aids to Gupta?"

"That's not my job, sweetie. I'm the strong outraged American. I scream my guts out. That's my job."

"But if you'd been to Gupta, you'd have seen the suffering. We have to do more."

"Hey, little shitheel, I sang my lungs out. You can't get no more out of this man."

"But the people aren't getting anything."

"I'm the voice of rage and justice, not the food-delivery man, baby. Get your act together. I got mine."

Some others thought it was terrible, but they had bookings they had to fill. And still others had attended the concert because everyone seemed to be doing it and they had never even known what the benefit was for.

Debbie Pattie was alone and she couldn't even reach Remo. But she knew she had made it through a hard world right to the top, and if she could nail the thieves herself, she thought, then Remo, the one man she wanted and couldn't have, would have to come and admit she was someone special.

The money, as it turned out, went to several places. Everyone made money. The auditorium management hoarded what little it had to pay damages to families of the injured and dead rock stars, the unions received special bonuses, and one dandy little tidbit was that almost half of everything collected went to

Gadgets Unlimited, the company that provided the wiring and lighting for the stage. The accountants told her the people who arranged this were brilliant and knew just how benefits worked, even understanding that money could be taken out as security for future bills.

"If you hadn't alerted us we never would have found this rascal. This is the best job of numbers manipulation we have ever seen."

Gadgets Unlimited was in Grand Island, Nebraska. Debbie wouldn't go to Grand Island to die, but she would bring Grand Island to her. She phoned the company and got a machine. But this was the strangest answering machine she had ever heard.

"Yes, I am an answering machine but I can answer your questions, hold conversations, and even give you three minutes of appropriate sympathy if that is called for."

"I want to speak to the employee who handled the work on the Save benefit."

"A tragedy, yes. But the Save concert also contributed to furthering the interests of stage delights."

"There are a few million dollars' worth of bills here," said Debbie. She looked at the printout on the marble tabletop in her hotel suite. There were electron microscopes, mass spectrometers, and enough scientific gadgets to outfit a space capsule.

"And every one of them going for improved and better sound, not only for today but also for tomorrow."

"But wasn't this money supposed to go to the poor people of Gupta?"

"Everything after expenses did go to Gupta, we are led to believe. I think they got the very latest in the 'ouchless' gauze bandage."

"Look, to me that's fraud. And maybe you can pull

off fraud against most people, but I got a friend, a good friend, and my friend Remo . . ."

As soon as the word was out of her mouth she heard a fast click, and live noncomputer voice got on the phone. She knew it didn't come from a computer because no computer could be so grating on the ears. It twanged like a rusty nail across a piece of concrete.

"Remo as in Remo and Chiun," came the voice.

"Yeah. Them. You know them?"

"Know of them? They're my heroes, little lady. My name is Robert Dastrow, that's D as in Data, A as in Arithmetic, S as in Silicone, T as in Titanium, R as in Robot, O as in Ohm, and W as in Wildebeest, heh, heh, sometimes I throw in an animal. I'm a card, you know."

"Look, is there any way you can return some of that money to the people of Gupta? If you'd seen them suffering, you'd know we should do something."

"Right you are, sweet lips," came the voice. "I think we ought to talk about it. We ought to talk about it some more. I'd love to give everything to Gupta, but I have to know what kind of person you are, not just some fly-by-night who wants a million here and a million there."

"I'm a rock star. I'm rich," said Debbie.

But it wasn't enough for Dastrow, D as in Data, A as in Arithmetic, and so on, and finally Debbie Pattie agreed to meet the man with the rusty voice.

Robert Dastrow looked as he sounded. As though he should be in some hardware store west of Chillicothe, Ohio. He wore a plain starched white shirt with pencils in the pocket, wire-rimmed glasses, and a crew cut. If Debbie wanted to cast the perfect class nerd, she would call on Robert Dastrow.

But if he was so backward, why was the conversation never going where she wanted and always getting strangely back to Remo and Chiun? You would think he had something for them and not her. He wanted to know what they ate, how she felt about their vibrations, how they made love (if she could be supposed to know such information). He wanted to know any strange things they might have talked about.

"Well, it was like a family fight that went on all the time, like. You know what I mean? Like the old man was really his mother, you know? Not his father. His mother. Always telling him he didn't do this right or that right. You know, a mother who's always bitchin'. A normal mother."

"My mother wasn't like that," said Dastrow.

"Well, maybe where you're from they're different. But he was like his mother. And they were always arguing, sometimes in English. Sometimes in Korean."

"Did the older one seem to know more than the younger?"

"The older one didn't like this country, didn't like working here. Thought they ought to go."

"And just what work did they do?"

"I dunno. Those two were as mysterious about that as "The Twilight Zone." A weird pair. Bunch of stuck-ups. Who do they think they are, right? Remo thought he was better than everyone."

"You had problems with him?"

"Everyone had problems with him. The nice one was Chiun."

"I'll tell you what I'll do. You seem like a dedicated person and this concert was for charity. There is one way I can make back my investment if I sign over all the equipment funds to the Save committee. And that's if you introduce my new electronic guitar tonight. Because if you use it, and everyone sees how good it is, then golly, I'm off and running."

"All of the money you took goes to Gupta, right?"

"Yessiree, little lady."

"Is the guitar heavy? I can't work heavy. I move a lot. I'm a dancer too."

"I'll make it light. It's got a lot of wires, though. It works sort of on your brainwaves too."

And thus Debbie Pattie in the prime of her career allowed herself to be strapped into the new electronic guitar. Electrodes were set on her scalp and on her wrists and ankles, and when she began to play, this arrangement worked just as well as it did on any other electric chair.

Debbie Pattie got enough volts while singing before her rock crowd to do away with half the capital offenders in New Jersey.

Remo heard about her death on the television show Chiun was watching as he was packing his things, one extra shirt and one extra pair of pants. The problem wasn't packing the shirt and pants, the problem was getting them into Chiun's fourteen steamer trunks.

To squeeze in Remo's clothes, Chiun would have to get rid of a sleeve of one kimono. He carried a hundred and fourteen with him for light travel in the trunks, and each one, Remo suggested, became at one time or another the most important one. Finally Remo pointed out that there was a high unlikelihood of Chiun needing one only for the Campobasso Festival of the Grape in Italy, since the Italians hadn't worshipped Dionysus since A.D. 200 or so.

"Just when you discard a piece of a kimono is when you need it most," said Chiun. "But all right.

Mutilate its beautiful wine essence. If you are ready
to leave this insane asylum at last, I will endure it."

Chiun was watching a soap opera he had loved in
the early and mid-seventies but one which now he
disliked for its filth and violence. However, on occa-
sion he would tune it in, and this time it was interrupted to announce another rock star was dead as a
result of the Concert of Death in which so many had
died to save the suffering people of Gupta.

The viewers were warned that the scenes might be
too horrible to look at. To avoid the horror, people
should not look at the scenes which would be shown
now, at the six-o'clock news, and the eleven-o'clock
news.

"This is the Debbie Pattie concert," intoned the
announcer, and intense noise and a heavy beat followed. Debbie's voice was barely a whisper, a whisper of talk, and then it grew louder, and her
multicolored painted face turned a reddish hue and
then she was screaming, and thrashing in the wires
of the electronic guitar. She rolled on the ground
screaming as the audience joined her in ecstatic yells.
The drummer picked up pace and the fans were
jumping in their seats. Some of them ran hysterically
up onto the stage.

When the song was over, Debbie Pattie stopped
convulsing and was still as the audience went wild.
Unfortuantely she remained just as still when the
next number began. Men in white coats ran out, the
necessary medical teams that always accompanied
rock concerts. Normally they were used for the
crowds. One of them placed a stethoscope over her
heart.

"It was only then," came the announcer's voice,
"that the fans realized, that everyone realized Ms.

Pattie was not singing, but had been electrocuted by a malfunction in her guitar."

Within minutes there was another interruption, and Debbie's manager said the song would be released as a single, calling it her best work ever. A writer for *Rambling Rock* magazine appeared, calling it "the most powerful, sensitive interpretation of a larger scope of the dynamic of the frontiers of rock than Ms. Pattie had ever dared explore before. It was bold, yet in full knowledge of its absolute sensitivity, combined with a tonal daring that went beyond known frontiers of harmonization."

And then there was the report that got Remo's interest. Half her money was going to the victims in Gupta, but with a special proviso: no organization would collect it, but it was to be handed directly to the poor people in cash.

"Ms. Pattie had been investigating the use of the Save concert money at the time of her death," said an announcer.

"She was all right," said Remo. "She was better than I thought. She cared. She really did. She smelled awful but she cared."

Chiun looked up, alarmed. He sensed the sounds of American lunacy coming at him, specifically Remo's. These whites shared that insanity that he found almost nowhere in the Orient.

"Let's go now," said Chiun. "We will phone Smith from Dakar, or Samarkand, or Calcutta."

"I'll phone him now," said Remo.

"Why break bad news right away? Allow Emperor Smith the kindness to still believe you work for him for a few more days. I will take upon myself the onerous chore of severing relations."

"No," said Remo. "It's my job. I'll quit it."

"No, my blessed son, great bearer of the thousand-year skills of Sinanju, glory of our House, allow me to do this delicate thing."

"Don't worry," said Remo, who knew Chiun would not be saying nice things unless he wanted something badly. "I'll handle it."

Chiun did not listen to the conversation. Instead he sadly packed both sleeves of the kimono for the Campobasso Festival of the Grape, the ones shaded to honor the god Dionysus. At least he wouldn't lose a kimono he might need. But when he would be able to free Remo from this insanity, he was not sure.

Gravely Remo returned.

"I can't leave now, little father."

Chiun nodded wearily.

"The whole country may be destroyed by those shysters Palmer, Rizzuto & Schwartz. Do you know what they're going to do to the money supply?"

"Do not tell me, lest I lose sleep."

"They've figured out how to get two hundred million clients and sue the government at the same time."

"What horror," said Chiun, folding his hands.

"But in doing so, they're going to wreck the government. I can't let them get away with that. Not after Debbie."

"Of course not," said Chiun. "What is one death alone? We must give them two."

"I know you're being sarcastic, but I believe every word I'm saying. I believe it deeply. I'm sorry."

"The problem was never that you didn't believe what you said. The heavens know how much I have prayed that one day you would learn that your body does not have to follow your tongue."

"I know how much you counted on leaving," said Remo.

"Would you mind terribly if you did not get yourself killed? Would you mind terribly acting like the professional assassin I trained you to be? Would you mind terribly killing Smith's enemy instead of getting killed yourself?"

"Of course not," said Remo, who knew that Chiun from the very beginning had railed against America's monuments to heroes who died in battle. To the House of Sinanju this only glorified getting killed, rewarding what should have been discouraged.

"There is a way we can win," said Chiun. "But I am afraid you are going to have to remember what I have only told you a thousand times a thousand."

11

Palmer was laughing. Rizzuto danced on the expensive table and Schwartz was on the phone simultaneously with his stockbroker and his Rolls dealer.

Their days of debt were over. They were going to have more money than they could spend, more money than Palmer could divorce away or Rizzuto gamble away, and even more money than Schwartz could brilliantly invest away.

"I am afraid to say it," said Palmer, bubbling, "but at last the world is turning our way. Nothing can go wrong. We've got the biggest client list possible. The right victims, the right victimizer, read money, and we're in position."

"Bless the name Robert Dastrow," said Rizzuto, kissing a gold chain around his neck where he used to wear a religious medal.

"I never thought of Dastrow as a good guy. I never thought he did anything benevolent in his life. But I take it all back," said Schwartz. "The man is not only all genius, he's all heart."

"He's decent is what he is, gentlemen. We have met the decent human being," said Palmer. "I didn't think they existed anymore. He knew we were in trouble. He knew we needed a big one to pull ourselves out, and he did it for us."

"You know our problem was that we didn't let him pick the overall situations, too," said Schwartz. "This man understands the law. From here on in, we follow. He's smarter than us and that's all there is to it."

"He's better than us," said Palmer.

"He is us," yelled Rizzuto.

"What does that mean?" asked Schwartz.

"I don't know. I'm a trial lawyer. It sounded good," said Rizzuto.

Twenty minutes before, all three of them had been considering filing for bankruptcy, except Rizzuto, who was planning to leave the country because loan sharks did not accept pleas of insolvency without trying to collect pieces of the body.

And then Dastrow had phoned. He was initiating another case.

But this time Palmer was furious.

"We got nothing from the Grand Booree. The thing didn't even go off. We sent staffers out there. Staffers have to be paid. We got warning fliers printed up. Printers have to be paid. And what did we get? Less than Gupta, which wasn't enough to cover your fees to begin with. So, thank you for calling, but you are interrupting a liquidation meeting," said Palmer.

"I'm going to make you rich. You never specified rich before."

"Do we have to? Why do you think people enter law, to exercise their gums?"

"I only followed orders before, or made suggestions. This time I'm going to make you the richest negligence-law firm in the country."

"What's the catch? How is it going to backfire?" asked Palmer.

"How much are we going to lose this time?" asked Schwartz.

"What kind of craps will show up on the dice?" asked Rizzuto, with the dourness of a man who has just lost his seventh sure thing in a row.

"Just wait one moment," came Dastrow's voice on the conference speaker box hooked up to the Palmer, Rizzuto & Schwartz telephone line.

"I'm waiting," said Palmer, who wanted to give this Midwest tinkerer not one more moment of PRS time.

"You should have a package out in your reception room. Have it brought into your office, but don't open it," said Dastrow.

"Certainly," said Palmer. Well acquainted with Dastrow's tricks, Palmer hung up the phone and called the bomb squad. He wasn't going to let Dastrow erase the only link to himself with one simple little explosion, not that Dastrow ever did anything that obvious.

The bomb squad cleared out the office and cautiously ran a portable X-ray scanner around the package, while men in Teflon armor jackets cringed outside in the hallway. But the picture on their screens set them laughing.

"An enemy didn't send you that package, Mr. Palmer. If he did, I wish I had enemies like that," said the chief of the bomb squad. "It's filled with dollar bills."

"Oh," said Palmer.

"He's up to something," said Schwartz.

"Turning on us at a moment like this," said Rizzuto.

"It's when you're down the world steps on you 'cause it can't do it while you're up."

Even the secretaries were moved by that little summation.

Remembering that Dastrow did warn them not to open the package, Palmer brought it to the conference room, past the old wooden desk from their storefront days.

Dastrow was on the phone in minutes.

"All right, now you know it's not a bomb," said Dastrow.

"Do you have us bugged?" asked Schwartz.

"Of course I have you bugged. And I'm not the only one who has you bugged. I've been protecting you for some time now from some interference from your attackers. But never mind. I didn't have to listen to you to know you'd have the package checked for a bomb. You think I'm running out on you and cleaning up the evidence. I knew you'd think that. You're still lawyers. You think like lawyers. You act like lawyers. You work like lawyers, at least most of them."

"I resent that," said Rizzuto.

"Shhhh," said Schwartz. "Go ahead, Dastrow."

"Yes, Robert, please do," said Palmer.

"I want you to follow my directions precisely. Call in a secretary, have her open the package and take a handful of what's in there."

"Money is in there," said Palmer.

"Right," said Dastrow. "Do it."

Palmer called in the best secretary in the office, the one who could spell. Palmer knew she was the one who could spell because a client once commented that this was the first letter he had ever received without a spelling error. None of the partners knew that because they couldn't spell either. No one ever got rich by spelling.

The secretary was a bit mistrustful at first but when she saw the new dollar bills, she grabbed a handful with thanks.

"All right, now what?" asked Palmer.

"First, don't any of you dare touch that money."

"All right," said Palmer, looking at the stacks of dollar bills. If they were his he just wanted to pocket a handful. Rizzuto thought of how they would look stacked in front of him at a poker table. Schwartz knew he could leverage that little box of money into a prime investment on margin.

"If you got that out in the street, would you refuse to take it?"

"Of course not," said Palmer icily.

"Now go out into your outer office and say hello to your secretary."

"What's going on here? I'm not going to a secretary. She's going to come in here."

"Won't work that way," said Dastrow.

"Don't tell me how my office works."

"Suit yourself," said Dastrow, and all three heard him whistle away the time while Palmer buzzed for the secretary who could spell. But she didn't come. Another one burst into the room.

"Mr. Palmer, she can't move. She says her hands feel numb and she's nauseous."

"I told you so," came the voice from the box.

"Who's that?"

"Never mind," Palmer told the secretary who had just entered.

When she had gone, Dastrow told Schwartz to take away the woman's pocketbook but be sure to wear gloves. He assured all of them their secretary would get better.

"But if she kept those dollar bills longer than a few moments, if she actually fingered them awhile, the damage would be permanent. She would lose her ability to perform good work, possibly even the ability to recognize loved ones, and she would never have a decent night's sleep again in her life. She's been poisoned."

On those words, Palmer, Rizzuto, and Schwartz began to understand the magnitude of their salvation.

"The United States government, through its carelessness, has printed money that is toxic. You've got the United States government as your target. It's got all the money in the world. You've got everyone who handles money as your client. You're rich."

And then the laughter began. Dastrow even explained how it worked.

"At certain times during its destruction, paper money is naturally toxic. I just made sure that certain people readjusted the formula for the ink so that it would be toxic right away. The new ink isn't in place quite yet. But now is the time to get yourself on the ground floor. Now is the time for you to start accusing the Treasury of sloppy practices, perhaps even hint at the poisoning of innocent victims, everyone who trusts the American dollar."

Harold W. Smith could not miss the signs coming from Palmer, Rizzuto & Schwartz. They were not only going to do it again, they were going to do it to America. But this time they made their biggest mistake.

At Grand Booree they had advertised they were coming. But in the new attack on the government

money supply, Palmer, Rizzuto & Schwartz had made
the fatal slip. Previously there had always been some
form of protection on certain calls. Smith could tell
when the blockages came up. But now these very
calls from that source that had to be the source of all
the accidents was open. And they had made the
mistake of communicating with the government printing plant in Nevada, the one just outside the atomic
testing range.

It was to this one that Harold W. Smith had ordered Remo, praying that it was not another trap like
the Grand Booree. He really had no choice. If money
could be made toxic, then there would be more than
a negligence case. A whole nation would be crippled.

And Remo knew this. He knew the dangers as
much as Smith. But someone, he said, had taught
him a lesson about courage. Someone, he said, who
had surprised him with her courage.

"We are not going down without a fight," he had
said.

Smith felt relieved until his computers started pick-
ing up trouble at the atomic range site. It seemed
that there was going to be an accident.

Robert Dastrow sat in his fixit shop, the perspira-
tion pouring from his forehead. He wiped his hands
several times on his slacks, and to take his mind off his
worrying he played with his personal cyclotron for
half an hour. But even that didn't help. He had
finally come up against something he couldn't understand. This time he didn't know how things worked.

He had seen the reactions of Remo and Chiun, so
he knew these were no ordinary men. But he realized they weren't mystical either. These two had
perfected optimal use of the human body. Normally,

less than ten percent of human physical potential was used in lifting and running. These two had somehow learned to use it all and maximize their power.

Everything Dastrow had done was done right. You examined something and then you fiddled a bit and then you knew how it worked. He had examined Remo and Chiun on the stage at the Save benefit performance. He had readouts that would have shamed an internist. Physically he knew exactly what they could do. They could do almost anything.

Then he did the fiddling. He tried them with guns, knives, and explosives, and that didn't work. So instead of fiddling some more he used what couldn't be dodged. A massive amount of water pressure, and the trap baited by triggering the patriotic urge of one of them.

It had worked perfectly even though it hadn't worked at all. They were better than he had thought. It was then that Robert Dastrow panicked and used a full court press.

He not only drew one of them to the atomic site, but he worked on what he had found out from Debbie Pattie. It was merely a tinkerer's kick at a machine. He was trying several things at once.

And so he waited, watching the clock and waiting for his machines to tell him that at least one of the enemy was dead. But the word didn't come. He made himself a peach milkshake with sweet marshmallow sauce and fruit sprinkles. He drank down the sweet goo, licking the faint pink mustache delicately from his lips. He had two more while waiting for Nevada to blow up. Instead of explosions he saw his machine answering someone, and then a red light when the machine indicated that it had a question from a caller it couldn't answer.

Robert picked up the phone, pressing a button for a fast review of the conversation. It was Chiun, the Oriental part of the two-part team.

"Here," said Dastrow. He tasted the residue of peach and marshmallow sticking to his teeth. He sucked it down his throat and rubbed a hand over his lip to gather the last traces of sweetness.

"Are you the voice that spoke to me from the walls of my motel in Booree?" came the high squeaky voice of the Oriental.

Dastrow checked his machines. The Oriental was no longer in Booree, but in Lockwood, Nebraska, less than an hour's drive away. That was a good sign.

"I have come to where you suggested. We have come for our payment. But I am afraid I am going to need more money."

"I don't know where you come from, sir, but when I make a deal, it's a deal."

"We too make a deal that is a deal. We have four thousand, five hundred years of deals that are deals. We have a tradition that I have told you to examine."

"Yeah, well, I have found you mentioned."

"Found us mentioned? Found us? Before your little bud of a country was born, we were. When Angles and Jutes scrambled over the barren cliffs of England, we were. When czars were just a future dream of some barbaric animal-skinned tribes, we were. We were before Rome set one stone to another, and you in this town of Lockwood which has barely cut the first layer of its earth dare tell me you found us mentioned."

"You've been around a long time. But I've problems too. I'm not just a voice that comes from a wall, you know. That's a device I use. I need people to work for me, at prices that are sound and reasonable."

Dastrow looked over at his monitors. Why hadn't the bomb gone? Hadn't the white man, the only thing keeping the yellow man in service to Dastrow's yet unknown enemy, gone for the trap? He had to go after all. Dastrow had found out that the organization the white man served was supposed to save the country. Couldn't locate it because they had even more electronic baffles than he did at this point. But it was clear that was how he worked and why he worked, and when Dastrow set a trap, just like a mousetrap it always worked.

But the bomb had not gone off. It was all but certain a bomb had to be able to destroy one of these two. After all, they were flesh. And nuclear blasts turned flesh to vapor.

But it hadn't gone off.

"Ah, but I have good news. I bring you my son, who has seen the light. We have truly been betrayed in the contract with our current emperor."

"Who is it then?"

"Will you pay for both of us? We do not come separate, but let me assure you the quality of the work is more than doubled. And your glory and your life will shine for many ages."

"How do I know it's not a trap?"

"Fool, we have been doing business for four thousand, five hundred years. Certainly that was enough time to betray a client, to break our word. Did you not check us out? Do you hire assassins willy-nilly?"

"I've checked you two out better than any men I've worked with. You've got to admit I have reason to be leery. After all, I tried to kill you, you know. I almost did it with the white guy."

"That's business. We are professional assassins. Do you think after four thousand, five hundred years we

take it personally when someone tries to kill us? You
know how things work. Can you possibly conceive of
us betraying a client and history not revealing it
once? Not once. Or were you lying to me when your
voice came from a wall? Do you wish to hire us or
not?"

"There was too much to read all at once. I fed it
into a computer, but I wasn't looking for betrayal,"
said Dastrow.

"Look for it," said Chiun. "I will wait."

Dastrow always had all his information stored in a
huge data base from which he could retrieve bits and
pieces whenever he wanted. The problem was that
the information on Sinanju went in with the rest of
the world. And unable to isolate Sinanju at first, he
saw centuries upon centuries of betrayal by everyone, but not one betrayal came up marked "Sinanju."
In all the histories of corporations, countries, and
leaders there was not one bit of evidence that Sinanju
had ever failed a client, although there were many
stories of gratitude by pharaohs and tyrants and other
rulers toward the assassins from the little village on
the West Korea Bay.

It made sense. The one thing of value in a dynasty
of assassins was, necessarily, Sinanju's reputation.
Otherwise they would be counted among the thousands, millions of petty killers throughout the ages
who had killed or were killed.

So that was how it worked. It was an unbroken
line through history. They naturally had to keep
records, and as they grew, their records made them
more knowledgeable about how the world worked.

And if the Oriental were going to double-cross
him, would he really be bargaining so hard for an
increased fee?

"I won't go double for two," said Dastrow. "The younger one obviously lacks the experience, skill, and general worth that you've accumulated working around the world. After all, you are the teacher, aren't you?"

"Yes," said Chiun and then spoke to someone nearby. "He made us a good offer, Remo. He understands us."

"I didn't hear him say yes," said Dastrow.

"He's emotional, but he'll get over it. He's still attached to the one he works for. You must know how we work by now."

Dastrow said he did. He gave them directions to his Grand Island laboratory. Actually, he did not know for certain how they worked. After he had made the deal with Chiun, he had picked up the return of Remo and Remo going into the shower. He was so shocked at Remo's survival that he thought he'd fouled up his bugging of their hotel room because he stopped hearing anything. But when the sound resumed as they left the room, Dastrow realized that physically they did what countries might do electronically. One of them, probably the Oriental, had sent out countering sound waves so that their voices could not be heard by electronic ears.

He was sure this was so because the first readout of their reactions showed they could by extension have just such powers.

Dastrow made himself another peach milkshake, and when he saw the two assassins arrive he buzzed them into his underground laboratory.

"Greetings, Master of Sinanju and pupil," said Dastrow. "I guess this just about makes me the most powerful man in this country."

He held out a hand, and promptly Remo caressed it into jelly.

Dastrow screamed. It was worse than the bullies back in high school.

"You lied. But Sinanju never lies. There are no records in four thousand, five hundred years," wailed Dastrow.

"We lie all the time, jerk," said Remo. "What do you think? We go around killing people and then recoil at a fib?"

"We don't lie," said the Oriental. "This was a tactic used by a Master We during the later middle kingdom of the Tang Dynasty. It is not a lie."

"We lied to him, little father. We lied through our teeth."

"What about your reputation? What will happen to your reputation?" sobbed Dastrow. His right hand felt as though it were melting. He would do anything to stop the pain.

"It'll be fine. We kill anyone who badmouths us. Reputation is great. You didn't find anything in almost five thousand years. That means no one lived to tell about the double crosses, the sneaky deals, the two-faced lies we've told."

"He lies," said Chiun. "He just likes to embarrass me. This is not lying. It is a legitimate strategy in defense of an embattled employer, turning down even more money than we were paid. And so it will be recorded that despite blandishments of all kinds and threats of death, the House of Sinanju stood by a poor and beleaguered client, because Sinanju kept its word."

"See what I mean?" said Remo. "Nobody else is going to be alive to know different. Actually, Chiun will turn on our organization the minute he knows he can pry me away. He got paid to train me, and he doesn't want to leave me."

"I want to get something back," said Chiun. "For all the years of ingratitude, I deserve something."

"Excuse me," sobbed Dastrow. "But I am in excruciating pain."

"I can end that, but I've come for something. I need evidence against that shyster law firm Palmer, Rizzuto & Schwartz."

"I'll give you evidence. I'll give you money. I'll give you a cyclotron. I'll give you anything. Please stop the pain! I know you two have control over bodies," said Dastrow. He fell to his knees and turned his head away from the throbbing hand. Just as he had figured, Remo could make the pain stop. If the two had control over their own nervous systems, they had to know where all the pressure points were. With enormous relief, numbness came at the end of his wrist. He did not look at what was left of the hand but let it hang by his side.

"Now where were we?"

"I was about to do it to your other hand," said Remo.

"Evidence. Evidence," sang Dastrow. "Glad you asked for evidence. I accumulated enough evidence to put those three away forever, or have them gassed in California, electrocuted in New York State, and garroted in Zaragoza, Spain."

"Gas would be fine," said Remo.

"Gassing is never a good death," said Chiun.

"But they are a California firm."

"Gassing lacks a sense of drama. Beheading has a good drama to it, but it messes the body," said Chiun.

"Well, all we have is gassing and electrocution,"

said Remo. "Oh, or death by poison injection now, in some places."

"The Greeks used poison. Hemlock has a nice ring . . ." said Chiun. "But use gas if you must."

"He's working on the histories. All of this stuff goes in. We'll take gas."

"Gas it is," sang out Dastrow, still avoiding even a glance at what he knew was no longer a hand.

When the printout arrived, spit like a long white tongue from one of the machines against the wall, Remo went over to read the evidence. He had forgotten much about what constituted evidence in court since his early days as a policeman, before Sinanju. But this read like a half-dozen airtight cases. Naturally Dastrow knew how the courts worked.

"Okay, look. I'm painless when I choose to be," said Remo.

"Is there any deal we can make? For my life I'm willing to pay twice what I offered for your services."

"Sinanju is known for mercy, if nothing else," said Chiun.

"No," said Remo. "You gotta pay for Debbie Pattie. You gotta pay for those poor people in the airplanes. You gotta pay for the people of Gupta."

"I'm willing to. In cash. In gold. In machines."

"No good in this market," said Remo.

"My lunatic son," moaned Chiun. "Into these crazy hands have I entrusted Sinanju."

Dastrow did not even see the stroke. He was waiting for one more response when suddenly all the waiting ended forever. He didn't see the darkness. He didn't even know there was darkness. He knew nothing, least of all how anything worked, except one last faint thought gone in an instant. And that thought was that the universe always exacted payment for crimes against it.

Nathan Palmer, Genaro Rizzuto, and Arnold Schwartz were all sentenced to death for conspiring to murder and for being accessories before and after the fact. In the courtroom each turned on the other with a ferocity rarely seen in the annals of jurisprudence. At first the prosecuting attorneys were afraid that these powerful lawyers from the all-powerful Palmer, Rizzuto & Schwartz might escape. But individually none of them could present a powerful case. Palmer had the overall strategy but could not quite get the law together to defend himself. Schwartz knew the tactics of law but came across to the jury as a man not to be trusted. And Genaro Rizzuto gave one of the most touching and heartrending summations ever heard in the courtroom. Unfortunately it had nothing to do with his case.

As the old saying went, a lawyer who represented himself had a fool for a client. On appeal, however, with new attorneys, the three managed to get their sentences commuted to life imprisonment. And then a strange thing happened. Somehow someone, reportedly a thin man with thick wrists, broke into their prison cells and released all three of the defendants. At first it looked like an escape, but it seemed this man brought them all to a little grove outside of Palo Alto where the families of some of the victims of the disasters had gathered, and there with heavy stones they together ended forever the most successful negligence firm in America.

At Folcroft, Harold W. Smith saw the overview of lawsuits in America. Remo had been only partly successful. He slowed them down for a few weeks. The trend had not been reversed.

In Gupta, Debbie Pattie's memory would outlast any statue or Hindu god. Before she died, she had donated a percentage of her income to the people of that city, specifically monies derived from the sale of her final record, the one she had died singing. "Help, I'm Being Electrocuted" sold more single records than any other song ever released in America. The video of her execution did not do quite as well. Viewers said that compared with other rock videos, it was too tame.

ABOUT THE AUTHORS

WARREN MURPHY has written eighty books in the last twelve years. His mystery and adventure series, *Trace*, received the 1985 Mystery Writers of America Edgar Award, and was twice nominated for best book by The Private Eye Writers of America. *Grandmaster*, co-written with his wife Molly Cochran, won the 1984 Edgar Award. He is a native and resident of New Jersey.

RICHARD SAPIR is the author of several novels, and lives in New Hampshire with his wife, Patricia Kathleen Chute.